BEAUTIFUL ASSISTANT

A CHRISTMAS ROMANCE (DIRTY NETWORK BOOK TWO)

MICHELLE LOVE

HOT AND STEAMY ROMANCE

CONTENTS

Made in "The United States" by:

Michelle Love

© Copyright 2020

ISBN: 978-1-64808-709-7

❀ Created with Vellum

BLURB

I'd spent my whole life knowing that there was only one man for me, but why did he have to be my boss ...

When we first met, I tried to deny the instant connection I felt to him. My dreams wouldn't deny it though, as fantasies took me to a world where only he and I existed.

I'd held onto my virginity, waiting for the one man I knew would come into my life one day.

Innately, I knew he would be the only man for me, but things were complicated.

Life had left him jaded, and now he couldn't see that what we had was what was always meant to be.

I needed him to believe, and I needed that to happen before it was too late, for someone else was out to ruin me.

He was my only chance to live out my dreams.

A life with one man, forever ...

"I would rather die of passion than of boredom."
Vincent van Gogh

CHAPTER ONE

Julia

New York, New York

Crisp January air hit my face as I got out of the cab in front of the WOLF television station, the newest network to open its doors in our fair city. Somehow, I'd scored an interview for the assistant position to the network's owner, Artimus Wolfe himself.

I had no real expectations of actually landing the job though. Fresh out of Columbia, I'd gained my bachelor's degree in Business Administration, but with literally no experience whatsoever, my chances were slim to none. The experience of interviewing with a man like Artimus Wolfe would be invaluable to me in itself though, so I jumped at the opportunity.

Nevertheless, I did plan on giving it my all. Adrenaline pumped through my veins as I walked up to the glass doors with "WOLF" printed across them. I shivered a bit, not from the cold air but from something else entirely. Excitement.

I wasn't sure why I was allowing myself to get excited over something I knew I didn't stand a chance in hell of getting, but there it was anyway.

Stepping through those doors into the warmth of the main lobby, I stopped and looked around at the grand entrance. A giant chandelier hung over the midsection of the large room. Not what I had expected at all.

Underneath that was the reception area. A young woman with short dark hair and thick, black-framed glasses stood behind a bar-like desk, her head bent as if she was reading something underneath the top layer of the desk.

Approaching her, I asked, "Do you know where I can go to meet Artimus Wolfe for an interview?"

She looked up at me. "Oh, hi. Didn't see you standing there. Can I have your name, please?"

The room was bustling with people, so I couldn't fault her for not realizing one of us had stopped in front of her. "That's okay. My name's Julia Bengal. I've got a ten o'clock appointment with Mr. Wolfe. I know I'm fifteen minutes early, but it's my nature to be ahead of schedule whenever possible."

"Cool." She picked up a pen and made what looked to be a checkmark on something before looking back up at me. "I'll need to see your identification, please, Julia."

Pulling my driver's license out of my purse, I handed it to her. She looked it over, wrote something else down, then handed it back to me. "Thank you." I put it back into my purse and looked in the direction she pointed.

"You'll take the elevator to the far left. You're going to the penthouse, so press the large 'P' button. You'll be in the lobby when you step off the elevator. Brady is the receptionist up there, and he'll tell you what to do when you get there." She winked. "Good luck, Julia Bengal."

"Thank you." Leaving the desk, I went to the elevator and felt that a knot had formed in my stomach. I was quickly disintegrating into a nervous wreck, something I hadn't expected would happen to me.

This was supposed to be nothing more than practice for me. Is this what I could expect with every interview I had? I expected to have many of them before landing a job. This was terrible news for me.

The elevator was full of people. It took forever for me to get up to the penthouse, and I was the only one left by the time I got there. I found it terrifying to be all alone in the large elevator. When it stopped and the doors opened, I saw another chandelier hanging in the reception area. Both of them were smaller than the ones on the ground floor, but more ornate.

A short guy was polishing the brass bar that ran across the front of his desk. "Hi, I'm Julia Bengal." I came to his desk as he walked around behind it, tossing the white cloth he'd been using into a waste bin.

Pulling off a pair of blue surgical gloves, he tossed those into the trash too. "You're early. He'll like that. Take a seat, Miss Bengal, and I'll let him know you're here."

Before my butt had even hit the chair, a man was coming out of the office right off the lobby. "Julia Bengal?" he called out to me.

My eyes caught his shiny black shoes first, and then ran up a pair of long legs covered in black slacks, all the way up his over six-foot frame. A white button-down shirt with the top two buttons undone rested under a black suit jacket. My eyes traveled over a firm jaw next, and a pair of chiseled lips smiled at me, and then my eyes finally landed on his—piercing blue, the smile in them as well. His thick, dark hair hung in loose waves just to the top of his collar. A broad set of shoulders and chest to match told me he had a lot of muscles underneath those clothes.

And there I was, ogling the man who was about to interview me for a job as his assistant. This was not good at all.

Why does he have to be so devastatingly good-looking?

My brain kicked in and my mouth opened as I walked toward him with my hand extended. "Yes, I'm Julia Bengal."

He gave my hand a little shake then gestured to his door. "Artimus Wolfe. It's nice to meet you, Julia. Please, come into my office."

The place was huge—so much bigger than I'd imagined. A dark oak desk the size of a dining table sat squarely in the middle of the room. Two black leather chairs sat in front of it. One more matching leather chair sat at the right of it, and a big, overstuffed black leather chair sat behind it.

I walked behind him and he pulled out one of the two that sat across from his. "You can sit here, Julia."

I took the seat he'd offered as he went around the desk to sit in his chair. "Thank you, Mr. Wolfe."

The nerves I'd had before were nothing compared to what was now going on inside my body. And what was worse was that my libido came to life in a way it never had before. My mouth watered to taste him, a thing that had never happened to me with anyone else.

I was a virgin, with limited experience in even making out. I'd had only one boyfriend in my life, though I'd kissed a couple of guys before him, but nothing ever went further than that. So the reactions that had been set off inside of me by this man were unusual and a little worrisome.

There I sat, looking at the desk. Only one paper was on it, and his hands quickly reached for it, moving it so he could read it. My head still in the clouds with thoughts of his attractiveness, I envisioned him wadding the paper up, tossing it over his shoulder, and looking at me with wanting eyes. Then telling me to get naked and get on top of his desk.

At that moment, if he'd said those things to me, I actually thought I might just do them.

But he didn't do that at all, much to my disappointment. "So, Julia, I see here that you're a recent grad from Columbia. But you're not from New York. You're originally from Atlanta, Georgia." He looked at me with a cute grin. "Now, how did a girl from Atlanta end up at Columbia?"

"I've always wanted to live in New York. I graduated from high school as the valedictorian and had several scholarships. I applied only to Columbia, which my counselor told me wasn't a smart idea. But I'd always wanted to go to that college. I put my heart and soul into it and was accepted. I've been on the dean's list since freshman year and graduated with honors." I went silent, feeling like I was talking a bit too much about myself.

He nodded, making those full waves of hair bounce a little. His haircut framed his face perfectly. He looked cute and yet still professional—a combination I'd never seen before.

He had to be in his mid to late thirties. He had that mature look about him, while still holding onto the young guy within him. And there I was again, ogling the man who'd be my boss—if I got the job, which I still didn't think I would.

"Being fresh out of college, do you think that gives you more of an edge than a person who has experience in this position?" he asked with a curious expression.

I had to ponder that for a moment before answering. "To be honest, I think there are pros and cons to hiring a person with experience. For one, they're pretty much set in their ways. And that might not go along with your ways, Mr. Wolfe. Yes, they know what they're doing, but will it be what you want? I'm a clean slate. You can mold me into whatever you want."

My breath caught in my throat as a vision of him physically molding me to fit with his perfectly masculine body zipped through my imagination.

Stop it!

"That's true." He looked at me as he nodded. "My last assistant had a ton of experience, and she kind of took over. She did the molding, since I had no clue as to what I was doing at first. It would be nice to get to do the molding this time around."

Does that mean that I have a real chance of getting this job?

Internally, I scolded myself for even thinking the errant thought. Of course I didn't have a shot at getting the job. The man was just thinking out loud.

"If I may ask, and I hope I don't sound like a fool to you, but what exactly would your assistant do, Mr. Wolfe?" I had to ask because I was clueless.

"Assist me." He gave me a big smile. "And not like make me coffee and bring me things, either. Help me come up with ideas to make the

station better. Deal with the things I don't have time to, both personally and here at work."

"Like making sure your laundry is sent out and taken back
home?" I asked. "That kind of thing?"

"No, my head housekeeper sees to all that." His long, thick fingers
tapped on the desktop. "More like a mind I can work with. Someone
who can motivate me, help me come up with innovative ideas, and all
the while keep the little things out of my way. Is that something you
think you could do, Julia?"

I had no idea if I could do any of those things. But I knew one
thing for sure: I sure as hell wanted to try. "I've got a lot of ideas
myself. I think I would be able to be all you needed me to be, sir. I
know I'd like to try. But I would understand if you went with another
candidate. Just having this interview is an experience that will help
me going forward in seeking employment and I have to thank you for
taking the time to let me do this interview with you."

He turned his chair sideways and crossed one leg over his knee.
"Your approach is different than any of the other candidates I've
interviewed. They all talked about themselves as if they had special
talents that no one else had. I found myself feeling as if I was trying to
make a purchase at a used car lot with annoying salespeople pushing
something I didn't even want down my throat. So, this interview has
been refreshing."

"Glad I could refresh you, sir." I had to smile at him, as his grin
was contagious.

I'd never had so many naughty thoughts about anyone as I had
over this guy—and all in the span of a couple minutes. He had it all—
charisma, charm, sexiness, and to top that all off, the man was rich as
hell too. Not that I cared about money, but who thinks having tons of
it isn't an attribute?

"I think we're done here, Julia." He got up and I followed his lead.
We began walking to his door as he went on, "I've got a couple more
interviews to do today, and then that's all of them. I'll be making my
decision soon. If you don't hear from my human resources department within the next three days, that means I've gone with someone

else." He shook my hand again after opening his door. "It was nice to meet you, and I'd like to wish you all the best."

"You too," I said, then left the gorgeous man, confident that what he'd said there at the last—wishing me all the best—meant I wasn't going to get the job.

Alone in the elevator, I sighed as my heart sank. I knew I'd never see that man again, and I'd most likely never step foot in the WOLF building again for the rest of my life.

I'd had no idea that interview would be such a rollercoaster of emotions, and I wondered how I'd make myself ever go on another one.

CHAPTER TWO

Artimus

My eyes were glued to her perfect form as she walked away from me. Tall, lean, and with just the right amount of curves, Julia Bengal was a walking heartache. Shiny black hair hung bone-straight down her back and bangs hung to her dark brows, framing her face, accenting high cheekbones. Coffee-colored eyes shone out at me as soon as I faced her. It felt as if she could see all the way through me, right to my very soul.

She wore sensible business attire—a black skirt that went below her knees, and a white satin blouse that she'd tucked into the waist of the skirt. A short black jacket made out of the same material as the skirt rounded out her outfit. Her lack of jewelry and her sensible flat black shoes told me she wasn't trying to show off her phenomenal looks to get the job she'd just interviewed for, but was simply being true to her style and herself.

As a matter of fact, she hadn't acted like any of the other people I had interviewed at all. I could tell nerves were coursing through her, but she'd managed to keep them mostly under control. Hell, the girl was just happy to have gotten an interview, being new to the workforce and lacking experience with the whole process of getting a job.

I knew I couldn't hire her though. Even though I'd looked through her application and found she'd graduated with perfect grades and even made the dean's list all four years of college. She'd been in the running from the start with those grades. But once I saw her and felt my body react in a way it never had before, I knew I couldn't have her around me as much as I would have to if she became my assistant.

And I found that to be a damn shame.

But my company had rules. Rules I'd come up with myself in the hopes of setting a better standard for our industry. Sexual misconduct wasn't tolerated. Dating between employees wasn't allowed either. And I knew the moment I saw her that I'd want to do more than just date that young woman.

A knock came at my office door. "Ashton here, Artimus."

I hit the button under my desk, opening the door for the producer of all our news shows at WOLF. "Come in."

He jerked his head back a bit. "Did I just see a woman coming out of your office?"

"You did." I leaned back and put my feet up on my desk. "I've just finished interviewing her. I have to say she's perfect, but I won't be able to hire her."

Ashton took a seat as a crooked smile filled his face. "If she's perfect then why can't you hire her?"

"Because I had an instant attraction to her is why." Looking up at the ceiling, I wished things could've been different. But they couldn't.

"Wow, how unfair is that?" Ashton drummed his fingers on my desk. "I think you need to think about what you've just said, Artimus."

I had no idea what he could be talking about. "And why is that, Ashton?"

He pushed his hand through his dark hair as he let out a long sigh. "You can't not hire her simply because she's attractive. It's not fair, not to mention a little sexist. That's almost as bad as hiring her just because she is attractive. Bottom line is, if she is the right person for this job, then you should hire her. And what is it that makes her so right for this job anyway?"

It was hard to figure out how to word it, but I gave it a shot, "She's raw. Willing to be molded." I rubbed my forehead as I thought about that. "In more ways than one, I'd bet." I looked at my friend for help. "See, I can't stop myself from thinking sexy thoughts about her. It would be disastrous to be around her as much as I'd have to be if she were to be my assistant."

Ashton seemed unfazed by my admission and he sighed once more. "Artimus Wolfe, would you please listen to yourself? You would deny that woman the job of a lifetime just because you think she's sexy? Hell, we've got tons of sexy women working here. You hired all of them. I've got to call this an unfair decision, boss-man."

I didn't like to be called unfair. I strove to be fair as much as I possibly could, at all times. What my esteemed friend and employee was saying got to me. So, I pleaded my case a little more, "Ashton, how could I work so closely with her without violating my own rules?"

"I do it all the time. You'll adapt." He winked at me, telling me he had the hots for someone he worked with.

My bets were on the cue card girl, Nina. The two often ate meals together, and I always seemed to find them laughing about something together. I'd even caught each of them sending some longing looks from time to time while the other wasn't watching.

But Ashton was a professional and knew his limits. He'd never jeopardize his career for a woman. And personally, he wasn't ready for a relationship; I could tell that. His past still held too much space in his mind and heart. A woman would only complicate things for him until he sorted that out.

My friend had something that held him back from making advances on any woman for the time being. I didn't have a single thing stopping me from doing that.

And Julia stirred me in a way that no one had since ... well, since ever. And if she could do that with just her presence for a few minutes, then what else could she stir in me when we were working closely with each other for hours and days at a time?

My assistant's primary work space was at my desk, just to the side of me. That way we could look at the computer together and see the ratings and things of that nature.

I knew that if I had to be that close to Julia for any length of time, it would become harder and harder to keep my hands to myself. And I'd have to do that if she were my employee.

It wouldn't be right to hire a person to work that closely with me, knowing that I have a hunger for her that might make me do things I normally wouldn't. Even as I sat there, trying to make a case for myself, I envisioned her lying on one of the sofas in the office, her skirt hiked up and exposing a creamy thigh as she bit her lower lip.

Shit, stop that!

"I can't hire her, and that's that." I slammed my fist down on the desk as if to punctuate my sentence.

"Wow." Ashton just sat there, looking at me with his mouth ajar. "How in the hell did she make that much of an impression on you with just a short interview?"

I had no idea. "You've got me. I felt some kind of physical spark run up my arm and through my body like lightning when I shook her hand. It took everything in me not to gasp out loud and throw her hand away like it was on fire. It was the weirdest shit ever, man. And she smelled so good—I feel like I can still smell her shampoo. I know I won't be able to control myself around her."

Ashton got up and walked over to the mini fridge, grabbing a couple of bottled waters. "Well, you might get mad at me, but I've got to say this." He tossed one of the bottles to me before taking his seat again. "You're being a hypocrite."

Okay, first he called me unfair and now he's calling me a hypocrite. This is too much.

"I'd love for you to explain to me why you think that, Ashton." I readied myself to take what he said into consideration before denying any such accusations against my person.

He took a drink of the water before saying, "You expect every single one of your employees to do what you don't expect yourself to do. That makes you a hypocrite. It's just that easy, Artimus."

Damn, he's right!

"So I am being unfair for not hiring a person who would be a great fit for the job as my assistant. Along with that, I'm being hypocritical by not hiring a person I have an attraction to because I've hired other gorgeous and great people to work here and have made rules that don't allow them to form relationships." My friend might be onto something, when I put it that way. I was being unfair and a hypocrite—two qualities I didn't like in other people. Those were also qualities I'd never realized I'd been harboring myself.

I supposed Ashton could see by my expression that the realization was hitting me, because he laughed as he got up. "Seems I've gotten you to see the light, but I've got to get back to work now. I just wanted to come see how the hunt for the perfect assistant was going. Seems the hunt is over. You've found her. All you have to do is get the hell over yourself the same way the rest of us have had to."

"Seems so." I watched him leave and put my head in my hands as I rested my elbows on the desk.

It wasn't easy to admit to myself that I wasn't the man I thought I was. I knew I had flaws. Everyone does. But I never knew I could be so blind to them.

There were more interviews to do. Julia Bengal might not make the cut if one of them made more sense to hire over her. Somehow that thought left me with a knot in my stomach.

I felt a smile creep over my lips as I thought about getting to see her beautiful face every workday. Hearing that soft voice—deep for a woman, with a side of sultry that I was sure she had no idea sounded so damn sexy and feminine—would be nice too.

Could I do it?

Could I hold back and maintain my self-control the way I demanded my employees do?

Shaking my head, I knew it would be hard. But I also knew that Julia Bengal was just the right kind of person to help me take WOLF to where I wanted it to be. The very top.

I wouldn't settle for anything less than that, and I needed the perfect person by my side to help me get it there.

Lots of late nights would be expected. Long hours, too. Hell, I was getting ahead of myself. She might not even accept the job once I offered it and let her know all that the position entailed.

But I knew I'd offer her the job. I knew she'd stay on my mind through the remaining interviews.

She'd already cemented herself in my head, it seemed. I prayed she wouldn't do the same thing in my heart.

A cloud of doubt surrounded me where my will and determination were concerned. But what could I do? I expected that out of everyone else. Time to face the music myself.

Why does that sound so damn scary?

CHAPTER THREE

Julia

The next day I was back at the job search, looking for jobs on my laptop. I had started bright and early in the morning, and by six in the evening I was feeling done with the whole thing.

I'd put in six applications at various jobs online, but the only job that really interested me was the one at WOLF.

I hated how I could get so single-minded sometimes. Just like with Columbia, I knew what I wanted and never gave a thought to any other possibility. And that's what was happening now with the position at WOLF.

I had no idea why that was happening in my brain. I didn't think I had a chance at all of getting even a second interview, much less the job. But still, I couldn't stop thinking about it.

Mr. Wolfe had said to give it three days, and if I hadn't heard anything by then, it meant he'd picked someone else. Well, it had only been one day, but at six o'clock I knew the office was closed.

One day down, two more to go.

My roommate came in, rushing to get to the bathroom as usual. She refused to use public restrooms. "Hey, Bethey."

"Hey, Julia," came her breathless reply before the bathroom door slammed shut, followed by a great sigh of relief as she finally got to pee.

Thankfully I didn't have as shy a bladder as she did. I couldn't imagine holding it in all day long.

Closing my laptop, I began to think about what I'd make for dinner when my cell rang. Picking it off the coffee table, I gasped, "It's WOLF!" Swiping the screen, I answered the call, "Hello!"

"Can I speak to Julia Bengal, please?" came a woman's voice.

"This is she." I bit my pinky fingernail as I waited to hear what she had to say. I couldn't believe this was happening.

"This is Tanya, with the human resources department at WOLF. Mr. Wolfe has made his choice for the position as his assistant. He'd like you to start on Monday. I'm going to need you to come in tomorrow to sign all the new hire paperwork, after I explain the job to you and you accept it, of course."

"Of course!" I put my hand over my mouth to silence the scream of happiness that was dying to escape. "Any specific time, Tanya?"

"No, just before five in the evening. I'll need about two hours of your time. See you tomorrow then. Have a nice evening and congratulations, Miss Bengal."

With the call over, I began to jump around my apartment, finally able to let out my excited screams. Bethey came out of the bathroom with a puzzled look on her face. "And what's this about, Julia?"

"This is about," I grabbed her hands and made her jump in a circle with me, "me getting my first job! I got the assistant job at that new network, WOLF!"

"No way!" She shook her head in disbelief. "You've been on one interview, and you've landed your dream job in less than two days. Julia, do you have any idea how rare that is?"

"I totally do." My head was spinning, so I stopped jumping.

Bethey pulled me in for a hug. "This needs to be celebrated. I say let's go out and get our dance on, girl."

I agreed, feeling ready to celebrate. We got ourselves dressed up and decked out, then headed out to one of her favorite clubs. I was never one to go out a lot. School came before anything else, and that had hampered my clubbing.

Whenever I had gone, I did enjoy it. The only drawback was that I'd met my ex-boyfriend at one of the bars that were popular with Columbia students—and that relationship hadn't turned out to be so great. But we weren't going to one that he frequented, just to be on the safe side.

Bethey didn't know the whole story behind our breakup. No one did. I preferred to keep that to myself. I wasn't particularly proud of myself for what had happened with the guy.

Bethey bought my first and only drink, as I'd never been a huge drinker either. I was a seasoned pro at making one drink last for hours. When you put your head into the books, alcohol proved to be your enemy.

We danced like no one was watching, as the saying goes. I loved to dance. I had no idea if I was any good at it, but I loved to do it. Bethey and I were dancing our little hearts out, and I felt like I was on cloud nine.

The music was rocking. The crowd was electric, and the night was going fabulously.

Until I felt someone grinding on me from behind and turned around to let the fucker know that that was not okay. And that's when I spotted my ex, smiling right at me, his face only inches apart from mine.

His soft blond curls bounced over his broad shoulders as he moved his hips in a sexy gesture. Bright blue eyes and boy-next-door good looks made him seem like the exact opposite of what he was—a great guy.

"What do you think you're doing, Price Stone?" I asked him as I stopped moving and crossed my arms in front of my chest. I'd worn a short romper that revealed a ton of cleavage and I didn't want him looking at it.

He had the nerve to put his hands on my hips. "Come on, baby.

I've said I'm sorry more than I've ever said it in my entire life. Can't you cut a guy a break?"

"No." I pushed his hands off me. "Leave me alone." Turning around, I tapped Bethey on the shoulder, as she'd turned away to dance with someone else. "I'm going to the bathroom."

She waved me on, and I left the crowded dancefloor. My great mood had been blown to smithereens by the man. We'd only dated for six months, and it had been a month since I had broken up with him—it defied my imagination why he thought I'd ever change my mind and want to start seeing him again.

How can a person keep seeing someone they don't trust?

It wasn't as if we were in love or anything like that. So why did he keep on showing up, calling and texting me, and telling me over and over again how sorry he was for doing something he claimed he didn't remember doing?

Just when I thought I'd effectively ditched they guy, I felt a hand on my arm, pulling me back. "You and I need to talk, Julia. This is the first time I've seen you in a month." There he was again, the asshole.

I glared at him. "Price, you don't even come to this club. Are you stalking me or something?"

He smiled that smile that had first attracted me to him. But now it made me kind of sick. "Stalking is an ugly word, baby. I just wanted to see you. I've missed you. Haven't you missed me at all?" His fingers tightened around my arm, reminding me again why I dumped his sorry ass.

"No, I haven't missed you at all." That was the truth. How could anyone miss a person who'd done something so wrong to them?

The way he looked into my eyes stupefied me. "Don't lie, baby. I know you've had to miss me. How many times do I have to tell you I'm sorry before you'll believe me?"

"You can't say it enough," I let him know as I jerked my arm out of his grip. "So stop doing it. If you'll notice, your apologies haven't done one bit of good. Frankly, I don't understand you, Price. You're a reporter for *The New York Times*. You've got your good looks and can be charming. So, what's stopping you from moving on and finding yourself another victim? I mean, girlfriend."

His expression changed to one of hurt. As if my words really had an effect on him. "Victim?" He shook his head sadly. "Julia, I don't remember what I did. I have to take your word for it. And I have. I was the one who woke up with a large bump on the side of my head, and I didn't see a mark on you. But I believed you and apologized to you and swore it would never happen again. Why can't you accept the fact that people make mistakes, baby? I am only human. And I don't want anyone else. I only want you."

He couldn't seem to recall that I had shown him the bruises he'd left on me. In the month since we'd broken up, I'd started to think that he only wanted me because of my status as a virgin. He'd nearly come on himself when I'd told him that the first time we'd made out and he'd wanted to take it all the way home.

My ideas about sex were different from most peoples. I'd always thought that sex was a lot deeper than most let it be. I wasn't religious, just deeply spiritual. I knew that sex with the right person could be a spiritual experience. One that made a connection between two people that would last forever—like eternally.

I knew most people didn't think the way I did. But I wasn't about to change my beliefs because of what other people thought. And I knew that Price Stone wasn't the man that I wanted to be with for the rest of my life. So he wasn't ever going to get into my pants and take my virginity the way he likely hoped he would.

It wasn't in me to be mean to anyone, but I had to stand up for myself. If I hurt the man in the process, that couldn't be helped. "Price, I don't want you. There is nothing you can do to make me want you. If you want to know the truth, I had no plans to ever have sex with you. Maybe that'll help you get over me. There would never have been any sex, Price. Do you understand that completely now?"

He shook his head. "You don't know that, baby. We were getting close. Hell, I'd finally gotten you to come over to my apartment. That told me you were getting comfortable with me. And that night would've led to more nights where you and I could be all alone in the comfort of my place. More nights where we could really get to know one another. I knew it would take a lot of time with you. I was ready for that. I was in it for the long haul, just the way you told me you would be."

He was taking my words out of context, which was something he excelled at. "I wasn't telling you that I wanted that with you, Price. I was just telling you that to let you know how I felt about sex. I'm sorry if you understood it differently than how I meant it. Yes, I was getting more comfortable with you, that's true. And just when I gave you more of a chance, you went and blew it." I gave him a good look over for a moment, thinking about my next words. "And it doesn't look like you learned anything from the experience anyways. You need to stop drinking, for one."

And just as those words left my mouth, the expression on his face jumped from sad and misunderstood, to one of elation. "I'll quit drinking. For you, I'll do that. I'll do anything for you, baby. You've got to believe me. Give me one more chance, please. I'm begging you."

A few people around us had become invested in our argument. I couldn't help but notice the women who looked ready to pounce on the good-looking, well-built man who was pleading with me for one more chance.

If I had real feelings for the man, then it would've bothered me that those women were waiting for me to walk away and leave him to them. There had been a part of me which had liked Price in the beginning—I never would've started dating him if there hadn't been. But a larger part of me had always felt that he couldn't be trusted. And that part of me had turned out to be right.

Looking into his blue eyes, I stuck to my guns. "Price, this is over, and it's going to stay over. Leave. Me. Alone." And then I walked away without looking back. Because when someone hurts you, you've got to have the backbone to not give them another chance to do it again.

CHAPTER FOUR

Artimus

When Monday arrived, I found myself feeling giddy for the first time since high school.

Julia would be coming in any minute, and my heart was pounding, my palms sweating, and I found it kind of hard to breathe. I wasn't feeling like my usual calm and cool self at all.

I'd left my office door open so that she could come right in. I wanted to welcome her to WOLF with open arms.

Adjusting my tie, I opted to take it off instead of continually tugging at it, as it felt tight around my neck. I'd dressed in a dark blue suit, and my pale pink button-down accented it well, but the pale blue tie was just too much. So I did what I usually did, pulled off the tie and undid the top two buttons of my shirt.

Feeling more like myself, I went to look out the window. The people looked like busy little ants as they moved about below. A New York street could hold my attention for a long time, with all the hustle and bustle that went on down there.

Not that I had hours to just stand there and look, but I was pretty sure if I did have that kind of time, I would stand there all day.

"Hello, Mr. Wolfe."

I closed my eyes for a moment, trying to gather myself. Her soft, sultry voice had already affected me. Opening my eyes, I turned to greet her with a smile on my face. "Hi there, Julia. You're about fifteen minutes earlier than I'd expected you."

She came into my office. Her long, dark, silky hair had been pulled back into one long, low ponytail. Her bangs fringed along her brow, accentuating her big dark eyes, the lashes naturally thick and heavy. Her lips were full and stained red, her high cheekbones accented with a bit of red blush, too.

Her navy blue suit matched mine perfectly. I had to comment on it. "Look at us. We match."

Her palm ran over her light pink shirt. "Right down to the dress shirt too. How funny. People will be thinking we planned this." She laughed lightly, the sound musical, the tones tickling my ears.

"I bet they will," I agreed, then led her to her office. "First things first. Let me show you your office." Pushing open the door that adjoined our offices, I let her walk in first to her new space.

"Wow. I can't believe this." She went to the bank of floor-to-ceiling windows that gave her a wonderful view of the New York skyline. "This is gorgeous." Spinning back to look at the rest of the office, she took in the matching sofas, made from Italian leather in a soft cream color. The stainless steel mini fridge, the set of shelves made from the same redwood material that her desk was made out of. "I don't know what to say."

"Well, you can tell me if you like it or not." I laughed afterward. It was obvious that she loved it. She was in awe of the place. "Those doors over there go to your private bathroom and a closet."

"I've got my own bathroom and closet too?" She clapped her hands and put them under her chin. "This office is bigger than my entire apartment."

"Well, you can't live here," I joked with her. "But you'll probably be spending more time here than at home anyway. I want you to have all the comforts of home while you're here."

I took a seat in one of the chairs that had been placed on the other side of her desk, watching her as she walked around, running her hands over everything. "This offers me much more comfort than anything I have at home."

"And what's that situation, Julia? Do you live alone or have room-mates?" I watched her as she moved about with a grace not many had, especially not women as young as she. Her application had said she was only twenty-one. I'd never seen someone so young who had so much poise.

Her eyes landed on mine as she answered my question, "I've got one roomie named Bethey. She and I are best friends, too. We met in college. She majored in journalism and works for a writer who works for *The New Yorker*. How about you?" The nerves I'd noticed during the interview were nowhere to be seen now that she had the job. I found that confounding, as well as remarkable.

"I have several homes—one in the Hamptons, one on 5th Avenue, and a few more vacation homes that are scattered about the United States." Thinking about how she came from Atlanta, I wondered about her family. "Did any of your family members move to New York when you did?"

Julia came up to the desk, taking a seat in the comfy chair behind it. "This is nice. So comfortable." She looked me in the eyes again as she went on, "No one came with me to New York. I came here alone. I'm the youngest of four children. Three older brothers made it pretty hard to get into trouble when I was growing up." She smiled endear-ingly as she said it, showing there was no bitterness there. "They're all married now, with families of their own. Only our parents live in Atlanta now. We've all made lives in other states, but we all go back home each Christmas. Other than that, we don't see each other much."

"Do you miss them?" I asked her as I ran my hand over my leg, wishing I could just reach out and touch her soft skin.

"Of course." She laughed. "I wouldn't be human if I didn't. Mom and I talk once a week, so that helps me. The thing is, they didn't raise us to stay in the place we were all born. Our parents helped us achieve our dreams and supported each one of us on our journeys so far. How about your family? What are they like?"

I didn't like to talk about my family situation, or lack thereof. But she'd been so open with me that it would've been rude not to share things with her too. "Two years ago, my parents died in a plane crash. I'm the oldest of four—three younger sisters. I've got aunts and uncles still, but we weren't that close to them."

She looked at me with an empathetic expression as she asked, "And why's that?"

"My mother came from a wealthy family." I hadn't ever told a soul about this part of my life. Funny how it didn't feel so hard to talk to her about it—and without her having to pry it out of me. "She was an only child and she inherited everything her parents had, which was a hell of a lot. My father came from a large family, which was anything but wealthy. It took his six brothers and sisters no time at all to burn their bridges with my parents as they asked for financial help nearly every single day for years."

She nodded. "So sad."

I nodded in agreement. "Yes, it was. And it was even sadder when my parents cut them all off. Every single one of them turned away from our family, calling us all selfish monsters—even me, after their funeral. It wasn't ten minutes after my parents were lowered into their graves that I was asked for the first hundred thousand dollars. Rushing my sisters to get into the car so they wouldn't be bothered, I didn't make it to the car before three more of my aunts and uncles asked for over a million more from us." I stopped myself, unsure why I was telling this virtual stranger so much about myself.

Her chocolate eyes took me in; I swore I could feel arms come around me, as if holding me in a gentle embrace. "That had to have hurt. It's a shame how people can be, isn't it?"

"It is." I looked away, breaking the unsettling connection that I'd felt between us as our eyes had locked.

I hadn't even heard her get up and move in behind me, so her hand on my shoulder surprised me. "Best to leave them where they are then. You're better off without them in your life. So, how about you show me around the station so I don't get lost?"

My head went light at her soft touch. And when she pulled her hand away, I felt lost for a second.

This is not good!

Shaking my head to clear it, I got up. "Yeah, let me show you around."

The walking would help, I hoped. I hadn't been ready for my reaction to her. I'd been preparing myself for the attraction I felt for her, but the connection was unexpected.

We walked out of her office, and I pulled her keycard out of my pocket. "Here, you'll need this to get into your office. Keep it with you at all times. But if you do forget it, then you can ask Brady to let you in. He's got the master, and he can help you out if you need it. But he gets snippy about having to do it, so we all try not to bring that out in him."

"Good to know. I don't want to make him get snippy with me." She smiled, and it took my breath away.

God, how am I going to do this?

I pointed down the hallway. "Those offices belong to our news anchors. Let's go down to the main floor and make our way up, and I'll show you everything in between. It might take you a little while to get your bearings, but the great thing is that most of the time you'll have me to guide you. We'll be working very closely so you won't be leaving my side much, especially at first."

"That's a relief." She reached out and pushed the elevator button, as she was closest to it. "I'd hate to get lost in this huge place and have to call for help."

The ride to the next floor, where other people joined us on the elevator, was a bit awkward. For me it was, anyway. Julia looked right at home already. We got our first comment on our matching outfits from Joe from maintenance. "So, did you find your long-lost twin, boss?"

"Ha ha, Joe." I took the chance to introduce the two. "Julia, this is Joe. If you find a mess or accidentally make one, you'll call him."

She reached out, and the two shook hands. "Nice to meet you, Joe. I'll try not to make any messes I can't clean up myself."

Joe took his job very seriously. "Miss, I don't want you to go getting your nice clothes messed up by trying to clean a thing. My extension is 411, and I want you to call me and let me handle the messes around here. No matter how small they are. You hear me?"

"I hear you, Joe. Let you handle that. Not a problem, sir." I liked the way she used the term 'sir' with the older man. Respect for others always went a long way in my book. Just one more thing I liked about my new assistant.

I had this odd feeling that the things I'd like about her would just keep stacking up. Most people would've been overjoyed that they'd found such a great assistant. But I was both thrilled and not thrilled by my increasing respect for my employee.

Julia had already managed to take hold of me in a way no one ever had. But it was the rules that I had come up with myself that made it impossible to ever act on the feelings that I knew would continue to grow. I could already feel them blossoming into a lovely flower—a flower that had thorns all up and down its pretty little stem. I just had to keep myself from touching the flower, or else I knew I'd get cut, leaving me bleeding and hurting.

CHAPTER FIVE

Julia

The tour had gone great, and the fact that I didn't have to worry about going anywhere on my own for a while reassured me. The offices were huge, so I was happy that Mr. Wolfe would be with me. But that wasn't the only reason I was glad to be around him—I'd discovered that the man had many attractive qualities, even more than simply his handsome face and muscular physique.

He was genuinely nice to everyone. He not only knew everyone by name, he also knew about their personal lives, asking one of the reporters how her sick aunt was doing. From the lowest on the totem pole to the highest, Artimus Wolfe treated each of his employees with respect, and that said a lot about him in my eyes. I found it enlightening to know that I would get to work with someone I respected completely.

Not in a million years had I expected a man with his great wealth and power to be so down-to-earth and real. I'd always been under the impression that rich people looked down their noses at others who didn't have the good fortune to have the kind of money that they did. But I'd been wrong, and I could admit that. Mr. Wolfe had proven that not all people of wealth were arrogant, stuck up, rude, and boorish. He was none of those things. No, he was better than I had ever expected.

We made it back to his office, and I made a suggestion. "How about you let me get all nosy and snoop around your office and mine to find out where everything is?"

He looked pleased with my idea. "Have at it. I've got a few emails to answer while you do that." He took his seat behind his desk and went to work on his laptop.

A swift knock came at his door, and a man called out, "Artimus, it's me."

I had no idea who "me" was, but my boss did. He pushed a button on the bottom of his desk and noticed me looking at him. "You have one in the same place on your desk too, Julia. The doors automatically lock when they close, so this eliminates the need for any of us to get up and open our doors when we have a visitor." He turned his attention to the man who came through the now-open door, and I instantly recognized him as the morning anchorman.

Duke Cofield co-anchored the morning show with a woman named Lila Banks. The two made a great team, and I loved the format of the show, which revolved more around the two of them talking about the news, instead of simply reading it the way normal newscasts were done.

"How cool," I mumbled about the desk button and the man who strode into the office. I'd never been around celebrities before, and I found myself a little bit star struck. Quickly, I got over that, as we'd all have to work together and this would be no place for silly fan behavior from me.

Mr. Wolfe introduced us right away. "Hey there, Duke. This is my new assistant, Julia Bengal."

I approached Duke, and we shook hands. "Nice to meet you, Julia."

"You too, Duke. You're part of the morning anchor team, and you do the sports on the evening news, right? I've seen you. You're great. A real natural. WOLF is lucky to have found you." I had to get back to finding out where everything was, so I turned to leave the gentlemen to themselves. "If you guys will excuse me, I have to snoop around to find out where everything is so that I can actually start helping the boss."

Mr. Wolfe offered Duke a chair. "Take a seat, Duke. What has you dropping by today?"

"Love," came Duke's response, pricking my ears. I wasn't trying to eavesdrop, but I wasn't trying to ignore the conversation either.

"Love?" Mr. Wolfe asked. "So, you've met someone?"

"I have." Duke let our boss know. "Okay, let me just get the rest out there for you. Lila and I are in love."

Lila was his co-anchor for the morning news, and I knew that was a no-no at this company. There were strict no-dating rules in effect at WOLF. I had no idea how our boss would handle this situation. I looked back to find Mr. Wolfe rubbing his temples. He didn't look pleased at all with this bit of news. "Shit."

"No, it's not bad. Don't say that. It's good." Duke paused and looked down, his expression somewhat defeated. "Or at least it was. It was great actually. Up until she and I broke up."

I found that sad, but Mr. Wolfe didn't seem to share my opinion. "Oh! So you've broken up. Okay, then. Things will be fine. You'll meet someone else. And I won't have to fire you both. This is good. Much better."

Poor Duke clearly wasn't feeling that way at all, and he shook his head. "No, Artimus, this is not good. This is anything but much better. This is awful. This is as close to hell as I've ever come. And believe me, I've come very close several times in my life. This is a train wreck, is what this it. We've got to come up with a solution, you and I. I need her in my life. I can't stand not being with her. And I know it's killing her too."

Mr. Wolfe waved his hand in front of him as if clearing the air of any negativity. "She's okay. I haven't noticed her performance lacking at all."

Duke sat back, crossing his arms over his broad chest. "Because she's a professional, Artimus. Have you even noticed her fingernails?"

Mr. Wolfe clearly had no idea where Duke was going with that line of questioning. "Um, no. What the hell does that even mean, Duke?"

"She paints them to match her outfit. Every single day, that woman puts on a new shade of polish, and she hasn't changed her polish in a week. Not at all since I broke up with her." Duke hit the desk, making me jump a little—even though I wasn't supposed to be eavesdropping. "That means she's depressed. Upset. And it's all over our breakup, which I didn't even want to do, but felt I had to if I wanted to remain sane."

Mr. Wolfe added, "And employed."

"Yeah, that too." Duke stood then and began to pace in front of Mr. Wolfe's desk. "Artimus, there has to be something we can do to be together out in the open and keep our jobs too."

For a long moment, Mr. Wolfe didn't say a thing. Then he raised one finger as if he'd come up with a great idea, a big smile on his face. "You could quit."

Duke looked as if he'd been smacked on the side of the head. "I'd rather not."

I couldn't help but feel for Duke, and figured it was time to step in and salvage this situation if possible. I understood the rules Mr. Wolfe had put in place, but there had to be a better way to handle things of this nature. I stepped up to join the men, trying my best to stay confident. "If I may be so bold, I'd like to say that losing Duke right now would be a terrible mistake. Just saying, boss." It wasn't much, but it was something, and it made me feel better than not saying anything at all.

I got back to digging through things, but my ears stayed pricked, listening to what the outcome might be and hoping for the best. Having to choose between love and your dream job couldn't be easy, and I didn't envy Duke or Lila over this dilemma.

Duke was persistent. "Artimus, there are legitimate couples who work together. I didn't sexually harass her."

Mr. Wolfe was quick to reply, "Good to hear. Now stop messing with her all together, and we'll be okay."

Duke's tone was solemn. "Do you hear yourself?"

"Yes." Mr. Wolfe paused before continuing. "I suppose I can't do anything if you two were, let's say, married?"

Married?

That seemed a bit to be a bit of a leap. But I held my tongue, hoping our boss would see reason sooner rather than later.

Duke strode toward the door. "Artimus, this is insane. You can't possibly expect me to ask Lila to marry me so soon in our relationship." From the corner of my eye I saw him running his hands through his hair, clearly agitated. "I guess I'll just have to quit then, if that's the only way to be with her." He stopped at the door, the brass knob in his hand as he turned to look at Mr. Wolfe. I had my fingers crossed that our boss wouldn't let Duke quit.

"So, this is my verbal resignation, and a written one will be on your desk within the hour."

Mr. Wolfe stood, shaking his head as he went to Duke. "No, you won't be resigning." He clapped Duke on the shoulder. "I'll rewrite the rules to allow consensual dating. You win."

Hooray!

Love won out again, and I knew morale within the staff would skyrocket with this news. It might've only been my first day, but even I had caught one or two people sending longing looks at a coworker during my tour.

Duke was ecstatic, laughing as he clapped our boss on the back too. "Thank you, Artimus. You won't be sorry, I promise." Then he was gone in a flash, and I had to assume he was hurrying to try to fix things with Lila.

My heart was swelling with admiration for the man who was my boss. "I don't want to overstep, but I think that was the right thing to do, Mr. Wolfe. I have to admit that witnessing that makes me even prouder to be working for you. You're a generous man with a big heart."

He walked back to his desk and took his seat, rubbing his temples once again. "I hope I haven't made a mistake. I mean, what if they break up and it ruins the morning show?"

"They're both professionals." I went around to the front of his desk to dig through a cabinet in the front of the room, so I could see his face while I talked to him. He didn't look as happy as I felt with the decision. In fact, he looked worried. "Didn't he say that he'd broken up with her a week ago?"

"He did say that." His expression perked up a bit. "And I couldn't tell a damn thing was going on between them before or after that breakup. You might just be right, Julia." And then a big smile curved his lips as he looked at me. "You are going to be good for me."

"I'm certainly going to try my best, sir." The way he smiled at me made my heart melt. If a friendly smile like that gave me goosebumps, then what would a more intimate, sexy smile do to me?

I had visions of falling all over myself if I ever became the recipient of one of those types of smiles. And now that the rules were changed ...

Who was I kidding?

My romantic fate didn't sit with this man. It couldn't. I was made for *one man only; I knew that at my very core. My heart and body would connect with only one man—the man. Artimus Wolfe could have any woman he wanted—and as many as he wanted, too. He'd never want the same thing that I did.*

To find true love and finally give myself wholly to that love. To find not just a partner, but a soulmate.

No, he'd never want the type of commitment that I didn't just expect in my personal life, but demanded. I'd never give myself to anyone if I didn't have that commitment. My beliefs ran too deep to forfeit them for anyone —even a man as extraordinary as Artimus Wolfe.

As I caught a glimpse of him, still smiling away as he looked at his computer, I knew these wouldn't be the last of my naughty fantasies about the gorgeous man. There was absolutely no harm in having fantasies, after all.

I was a mere mortal woman. I'd abstained from having sex with anyone for twenty-one years, but masturbation and fantasizing weren't off limits. A girl had to have her relief, or she'd go crazy.

CHAPTER SIX

Artimus

The lunch hour had arrived, and I found myself asking Julia to join me for lunch. She didn't know anyone but me yet, and I thought it wouldn't be nice to leave her on her own just yet.

She'd sifted through my entire office, finding out where everything was. She'd been crouching, looking under a cabinet in the back of the office. She got up, blowing her bangs as she did. "Whew, okay, I've got this room figured out."

"And now it's time for a lunch break." I got up and put the jacket of my suit back on. "There's a café just down the block. Lunch is on WOLF today, Julia."

She put her jacket on too, and then we headed out. "This is a nice surprise, sir. Thank you."

Though I liked that she was being respectful, the *sir* and *Mr. Wolfe* thing weren't sitting well with me. So, I decided to change that up. "Julia, you don't have to call me by my last name or sir. Call me Artimus. Everyone else does."

She nodded. "Okay, as long as everyone else does then I won't feel odd calling you that. Thank you, Artimus."

Somehow, the way she said my name sent chills through me. I supposed it was that sultry way that she spoke—which she didn't seem to realize was sexy as hell—that made it sound better coming out of her mouth. "Sure, Julia."

We made light chitchat as we walked to the café. When we got inside, I spotted Ashton and Nina, another of our employees, sitting together. I leaned in close to Julia to whisper, "Now that relationships will be allowed at work, I have a feeling that these two will come clean about having one. I see them together more often than not."

A smile lit up her pretty face. "Then it should be fun telling them about the changes, shouldn't it?"

"It should." I led her to the table to join them, as they sat at a table for four. "Hey, you two. Care if we join you?"

"Have a seat," Ashton replied, gesturing to the empty chairs.

"First, let me introduce the two of you to my new assistant, Julia Bengal. Today's her first day." I nodded in Nina's direction. "Julia, these are Nina Kramer and Ashton Lange. She's in charge of the cue cards, and he produces the news shows."

Julia shook their hands, telling them how nice it was to meet them both before taking her seat across from me. "I have to say that, so far, everyone I've met has been so nice. I'm excited to be working with all of you guys."

I couldn't help myself. The words spilled out of my mouth, "And I'm excited to be working with you, Julia. I know this is your first day, but we'll have to work a bit late this evening to get those changes made and emailed to each one of our employees before the workday starts tomorrow."

Ashton looked puzzled. "Changes?"

"Some pretty big changes," I told him, grinning like a maniac.

Ashton and I were pretty close, and he'd never let on that he might think of Nina as anything more than a friend. Sure, he'd had some experiences in his past that might've been stopping him from pursuing the woman, but he'd be free of the station's rules, if that's the path he wanted to take.

The guy was a hard man to read. In the beginning, he'd told me that he'd had a bad breakup with a woman who had only been after money. For a long time he'd left out that there had been another relationship after that horrendous one. He'd only let me and Duke in on that information last week. And it was that more recent relationship that had really affected him in a bad way.

"How big?" Nina asked me as she sat up, getting very interested in the topic of our conversation.

"Pretty big," I admitted. "You see, it came to my attention today that the dating rules may be a little too extreme."

Nina was quick to react. "It's not that extreme, Artimus. Lots of businesses have that same policy. It is hard to work with someone once you've broken up, you know."

Maybe she wouldn't be as happy about my news as I thought she'd be. I went on anyway. "It will still be up to each individual whether they think a workplace romance is a good idea or not, but I'm changing the wording of the policy to allow dating between WOLF employees." I waited for Ashton's reaction, and when I got none, I began to wonder if the relationship between he and Nina really was only platonic after all.

Ashton nodded. "Did this come about because of Duke and Lila?"

Julia gasped. "You knew about them?"

He chuckled. "Duke and I are pretty close. As a matter of fact, Artimus, Duke and I have become very good friends." He turned to look at me. "Frankly, Artimus, I'm kind of surprised you didn't see that coming from him."

With a shrug, I had to admit, "I just didn't see it. I suppose I'm not great at reading what's going on behind the scenes. Anyway, by tomorrow morning, you'll all have that information in writing in your inbox, and that means Julia and I have a lot of work to do."

Nina looked at Julia with wide eyes. "Your first day and you're already working late. Is there a significant other who'll be waiting for you at home, Julia?"

She shook her head. "My roommate is the only one who'll be wondering where I am. I'll shoot her a text to let her know, so she doesn't worry about me. She's a bit of a worrier."

Without giving it a second thought, I told Julia, "Let her know I'll be taking you home when we're done. No subways, buses, or cabs for you when you work late. I don't want anything to happen to you. You're quickly becoming my right hand, Julia."

"That's nice of you, but not necessary. I'd hate for you to have to go out of your way," Julia tried to insist.

But this was something I wasn't going to budge on. "Nonsense. I've got a driver and a town car, and it won't be any problem at all. Your safety means more to me than having to go out of my way, anyway. This will be the rule from now on. If I keep you late at work or any one of my homes, then I will see to getting you back home safe and sound."

She nodded and smiled slightly at me. "That's very nice of you, Artimus. I won't balk about it anymore. I can see it's important to you."

It was. I couldn't put my finger on it, but I felt like she needed to be protected. As if some instinct was letting me know that there was an unknown force was out there, waiting to grab her and hurt her in some way.

I almost laughed at my absurd thought. I'd never thought of myself as psychic in any way. But there was just something about her that spoke to me, telling me to be good to this person and watch out for her.

Having three younger sisters, I wondered if it was her status as the baby of her family that made me feel so protective. She'd said she had grown up being protected by her brothers, so maybe some older-brother instinct in me was rearing its head to take over that role. Whatever it was, I couldn't seem to help it.

The waitress came to take our orders, and I let Julia go first. "A salad, Russian dressing on the side, and a water, please."

That wouldn't be enough to feed a bird. "And what else, Julia? You've got to eat more than just a salad. How about some pasta or pizza? Maybe a cheeseburger?" I couldn't stand the thought of her being hungry, and I didn't know how else to try to get her to eat more, because this was yet another feeling I'd never experienced with anyone else.

"I don't eat many carbs," she told me. "I wasn't always this thin. I've got to work at it," she said with a little smile, letting me know she wasn't bothered by my ham-fisted attempts at trying to get her to eat more. She looked at the waitress. "Can you add a roasted chicken breast to the salad?"

Well, it was better than nothing.

I ordered a burger and fries and began to wonder why Julia seemed to have some body esteem issues. She was perfectly proportioned. Size D breasts, if I was correct, and a thin waist that looked perfect for holding while dancing. A healthy ass, round and perky. I knew I shouldn't be thinking about her like that, especially with all of my thoughts and rules on workplace harassment, but I just couldn't help it.

"We've got a gym at work," Nina was quick to point out. "I've needed a workout partner. If you exercise, you can eat more of the good stuff. That's what I do. Not that I'm in prime shape, but my clothes fit."

"You're in great shape, Nina," Ashton was quick to say.

She blushed as she shook her head. "I'm not, but that's nice of you to say."

"I mean it." He leaned forward to look at her and make her look back at him. "Hey, look at me." She raised her head and looked him in the eyes. "Don't ever knock yourself. You're a beautiful woman, and you're better off if you accept that fact, Nina."

As I watched their exchange, it was hard for me to determine their real feelings about one another. On the one hand, Nina's blushing told me that she was attracted to Ashton. On the other, Ashton was acting as any good male friend would, and not anything more than that.

What was even harder was remembering that I wouldn't have to be so vigilant about watching out for certain things, like my employees getting too personal with each other—as long as it was consensual and above board. With the rule change, I wouldn't have to monitor them nearly as much as I had been.

And as I looked across the table at Julia, watching her on her phone, I knew it was all because of her that I'd had a change of heart.

While Duke was pleading his case to me, Julia kept drawing my attention. Making me think about not being able to talk to her the way I might want to someday. Touch her the way I knew I wanted to even then. Make her mine in every way there was.

Make her mine?

Since when had I wanted to make anyone mine?

I'd dated plenty of women and never found one of them that I wanted to be around for any length of time. My mother had been on me to find someone and settle down and follow in the steps of two of my sisters. Mom had gone on about how Mandy and Macy had already given them four lovely grandchildren, and she'd always assumed it would be me who would have the first grandchild, and I hadn't given her even one.

Angela, at twenty-two, was still young enough when they'd passed away to have avoided our mother's well-meaning nagging about getting more grandkids. But Angela and I were very similar.

We were fun-loving, carefree, happy-go-lucky individuals who were always looking for what was around the corner, instead of checking out what was right in front of us. But now, all of a sudden, I was looking at what was right in front of me. And it made me forget completely about anything that might be around the corner.

The girls were talking amongst themselves, and Ashton leaned over to whisper, "And how's this new assistant thing going? Is she anywhere near the league of Mrs. Baker?" he asked, referring to my old assistant, who had quit after a health scare.

"Not at all, Ashton." I caught Julia smiling, and it stirred something deep inside of me. I wanted to see her smile all the time. I'd make sure to try to keep a smile on her beautiful face. "Julia is in a league of her own, and I wouldn't have it any other way. She's really the most perfect person to be my assistant. I do believe I'll achieve great things with that woman by my side."

He laughed quietly. "You're talking about her as if she's your wife, Artimus."

Was I?

CHAPTER SEVEN

Julia

It was a couple of days into the new job and I couldn't have been happier. Artimus and I were getting along like peas and carrots. I got along with every new staff member I met. It was as if I was meant to be there at WOLF.

A rap on my office door had me pushing the button to see who it was. It was my first visitor, and I was a little excited about that. I looked to the doorway and there stood Lila Banks. She hadn't been in until that day, and she'd come to meet me first thing. I was impressed with her already.

Her smart pale pink suit, her blonde hair pulled back into a low pony, and her signature matching lips and nails told me that she and Duke had indeed made up, and that she was back on top of the world.

She came in with a smile on her face. "Hi, I'm Lila Banks."

Hopping up, I went to meet her halfway and shook her hand. "Oh, I know who you are, Miss Banks. I'm Julia."

Her head cocked to one side. "Miss Banks? No, no, no. Lila."

"Lila," I said, and then held out my arm in gesture to the chairs by my desk. "Care to take a seat?"

She shook her head. "No, I actually came to get you. Nina is in my office, percolating magic, and I wanted to invite you in for a cup of heaven and some female gossiping."

My first invite!

"Sure, thanks so much for inviting me." I went along with her to the far end of the long hallway. Her office was at the very end, and I couldn't help but notice that Duke's was right across from hers.

"Here we are." Lila slipped the keycard through the detector, then in we went.

The smell of fresh coffee hit me square in the nose. "Yum, it smells so good in here."

Nina stood by the coffee machine. It was one elaborate appliance, but she seemed right at home with it. "Hey, you. How's the new job going?" Nina greeted me.

"It's beyond amazing. Even in my wildest dreams, I've never dreamt about this being the thing I would do for a living." I knew I was gushing, but I didn't care. "And my boss is the best person in the entire world. He's just so …" I couldn't find the exact word for what Artimus was.

Lila laughed. "I think you're looking for the word 'perfect,' Julia."

With a shrug, I agreed, "Yep, that's about the only way to describe the man." Lila pointed to the two pale blue leather sofas that were near where Nina was preparing the coffee. I followed her, taking a seat and leaning back. "This place is so plush. I hate going home each day."

"Right?" Nina agreed. "I mean, my little office isn't nearly as nice as these are up here, but I love my little space with the view of the city. Plus, Lila's been kind enough to let me chill in her office when I need some quiet time to myself."

"Pretty sweet deal," I said, then shook my head. "Sorry I can't offer you asylum in my office. It's connected to the boss's, and he might get mad." I laughed. "Who am I kidding? Artimus Wolfe never gets mad, does he?"

Nina shook her head as she poured rich, dark coffee into the bottom of three cups. "I'm not going to chance it. You know what they say about those nice types. They're nice only until you tick them off. And I'm not going to risk ticking off our boss-man at all. I love my job, and I love how well we all get along."

Lila was all smiles, and I just had to ask, "So, you and Duke back together, Lila?"

She nodded. "Yes! And it's so great to have our relationship out in the open. It was such a struggle before." She wagged her finger at me. "Duke tells me that you were an integral participant in the conversation he had with Artimus. He thinks that had you not been there and offered your advice, Artimus would've let him go."

"I don't know." I didn't want to take credit for Artimus making what I considered to be the right decision.

"I do," Lila said as she nodded. "I've seen a change in our boss since you started working with him."

"Yeah, he's more laidback," Nina added, then handed me the first cup of coffee. "Here ya go, Julia. Tell me what you think."

Cinnamon, brown sugar, and thick cream combined with the coffee to create a bevy of taste that blended so well together, it defied imagination. "Oh, God! This is the best thing I've ever tasted, Nina. I'm not kidding. This is amazing."

Lila took her cup, sipped it, then closed her eyes as she let herself savor the drink. "Ah." Her eyes fluttered open. "Our Nina here was a barista before she came to WOLF. What a godsend, huh?"

I had to nod in agreement. "You know I'm part of your pack now, right? The coffee has reeled me in. You won't be able to get rid of me now."

"Good," Lila told me with a wink. "Because three is better than two. Us girls have to stick together."

Nina took a seat on the other end of the sofa I sat on, Lila sat across from us, and we drank in silence for a minute, taking the time to enjoy the creamy concoction before jumping into conversation. I knew instinctively that I'd love hanging out with these women.

"So, who has any good gossip?" Nina asked.

"I don't know if this is considered gossip or not," I said as I wrapped my hands around the warm cup to embrace the goodness. "But Artimus was sure you and Ashton would come clean about already being a couple, Nina. He told me he sees you two together more than he sees you apart. So, what gives, girl?"

Her dark blonde hair bobbed around her face as she shook her head. "Hell if I know. The man is a mix of actions that I don't understand at all."

Lila was looking a bit tight-lipped, which I thought was kind of odd. But I didn't really know her yet, so who was I to say anything about it?

So I asked Nina, "What kinds of actions?"

Nina leaned up and put her coffee cup on the coffee table between the two sofas. "Okay, I've caught him looking at me. He's spoken to me in ways that make me think he likes me. But then two seconds later, he's going out of his way to act like we're just friends, even going so far as to play-punch me in the arm like I'm his pal or some shit. And then he's always calling out to me when he's heading out to grab a bite, telling me to come with him."

"Clearly, he likes your company." I tapped my fingers on the cup I held. "But that does sound a little confusing. I have to admit, when I first met you guys at lunch on my first day, I noticed things between you two. It seemed as if you'd known each other for a long time. And he clearly thinks you're beautiful, too."

"Yes, he does. That slips out of his mouth often, believe it or not." Nina looked confused. "So, if he says those things to me, and looks at me the way he does at times, then why is he keeping himself in the friend zone?"

Lila looked like she wanted to say something, and I caught her opening her mouth before snapping it shut and taking a drink. Nina noticed her odd reaction too, then looked at me as she jerked her head toward Lila.

I took the hint. "So, Lila, what's your take on the Ashton situation?"

Her blue eyes darted back and forth between us. "Can you two swear to me that what I tell you will never leave this room?"

Now I was intrigued, and so was Nina, obviously. "You've got our solemn promise, Lila," Nina replied. "What do you know about Ashton Lange that I don't?"

"Not that long ago, Duke told me something, but he told me not to tell anyone." Lila put the coffee cup down and gave us each a stern look. "So, if this gets out, I'll know why. You got me, girls?"

"I got you," I said.

Nina agreed. "Me too. Come on, Lila. You've got my wheels going. What's up with Ashton?"

Lila was finally going to let us in on the big secret. She sat back and laced her fingers together, resting them on her lap. "About two years ago, Ashton was engaged to a woman."

Nina gripped her stomach. "What? Why wouldn't he tell me something like that? We've talked about so much. I just can't imagine him not saying a thing about that. I mean, he told me his last relationship left him cold on dating. He said she was a liar and a cheat and only wanted him for his money. Is that the fiancée, Lila?"

Lila shook her head. "That woman was before the fiancée. Ashton doesn't like to talk about his fiancée. And he's got good reason, too."

Nina was thoroughly confused. "Lila, cut to the chase already. I'm over here letting my imagination go to some crazy places. Like, what if Ashton is a woman beater or a cheater or something? Why else wouldn't he tell people about her?"

"He's not a bad guy, Nina," Lila assured her. "Unfortunately, he thinks he is one. You see, the two of them had been engaged for six months after dating for only three months. They were on a trip to upstate New York. He was driving, and it began to rain. The road got slick, and he lost control of the car. They careened into the median. It was covered in trees, and he hit one."

My hand flew to cover my gaping mouth. "She was killed, wasn't she?"

Lila nodded. "And he blames himself for that."

Nina went pale. "My God. That poor man."

I thought the same thing. And I also thought he needed some help to stop blaming himself for an accident he had no control over.

"Nina, if you really care about that man, then you need to stop waiting for him to make a move. You need to go to him."

Lila nodded. "I agree. I don't think Ashton will ever allow himself to have you in his life the way you both want. He's too guilt-ridden. And worse." She looked at us with such sorrow in her eyes. "He told Duke that he has nightmares about it at least once a week. He can't stop reliving that terrible night in his dreams."

My heart clenched. I felt so much sorrow for the man. But I knew the love of a good woman could make miracles happen. I'd seen it before.

My own mother had saved my father from a life of loneliness. He was a Marine who'd seen too much over the span of three separate tours. He was a drunken mess when she met him, using alcohol as a way to hide from the horrors that filled his mind. She helped him, and with her help, they were able to find him even more help, psychological help. He'd needed her to get him on that right path toward professional help, and things got better for them both.

"Nina, do you think that's something you can manage in the beginning of a relationship?" I asked her. "Because it will take a person with tremendous strength to help him."

She shook her head. "I have no idea if I can be the woman he needs." She looked at Lila. "Thank you for telling me about that. It all makes much more sense now. The man is hurting."

"But no one is broken beyond repair, Nina," I offered.

She only shook her head again. "I'm not sure if I'll be able to do that. I've always been the type to let the man make the first few moves. I don't even know how to take the lead. And I sure as hell don't know how to help someone who has suffered such a tragedy. I can be his friend, but anything more than that might be a bit too much for me."

My heart ached for her and Ashton, now that I knew so much more about him. I'd always been an empathetic person. It was hard on me at times, feeling so much emotion from others.

Empathy was a gift and a curse, especially when you couldn't control a damn thing that happened to the people around you.

CHAPTER EIGHT

Artimus

After tapping on the door between our offices, Julia came into mine carrying a cup with steam coming off the top of it. "I've brought you heaven in a cup. You've got to try this. Our little Nina was a barista before gracing us with her presence here at WOLF." She handed me the cup, then watched me as I took a sip.

I wasn't into fancy coffees, or at least I thought I wasn't. When I tasted that creamy perfection, though, I became a changed man. "My Lord, this is delicious" I took another sip and knew if it had been even a few degrees cooler, I'd have chugged it down like a cold beer on a hot summer day.

"I know, right?" She was quite pleased with herself. "Lila invited me down to her office to have some coffee and chitchat with her and Nina. They're so nice. The minute I tasted it, I knew you'd love it too. I'll make sure to grab you a cup each time I visit her office."

"How nice of you." I watched her as she leaned over my desk to open the laptop. Her body stretched across the space, the curve of her breast drawing me in.

If I could only touch her.

I closed my eyes, pretending to be enjoying the coffee instead of trying to cool down my throbbing cock.

"Look here, Artimus." Her sexy voice forced me away from my endeavor. She pointed at the computer screen. "The ratings are high for all the news shows, with the exception of the afternoon news."

"I think that's to be expected. There aren't many viewers wanting to watch the news at noon." I placed the cup on my desk and tried to ignore how great she smelled, her nearness making her scent hover right next to me.

When she leaned down, her face inches away from mine, I looked at her bone structure, which I often caught myself doing. With her dark hair and tall frame, I'd often wondered something about her.

She stood back up and tapped her chin with her finger. "We need to come up with some ideas to bring those ratings up."

"Can I ask you something, Julia?" I wasn't sure if my question would be considered rude or not, but I had to know, for some reason.

"Sure." Her smile did it to me again, made my heart swell.

I tried to ignore that too. "Do you know if you have any Native American blood flowing through your veins?"

She laughed as she nodded. "I happen to have a good amount of Cherokee in my veins. My mother's mother was a full-blooded Cherokee. She married an Irish man, and my mother was their first-born. She tells me all the time how much I look like my grandmother."

"I'd love to meet her and your grandfather." I'd had no idea that was going to come out of my mouth, but it had.

She turned away from me, her head bent a bit. "I wish you could. They've both been gone for some time."

How stupid of me.

I got up, feeling bad for bringing up something that would make her sad. "I'm sorry, Julia. I didn't mean ..."

She turned back with that smile on her face again. "Don't be sorry. They lived long and good lives. I'll see them again when it's my time to join them."

She was remarkable. "You've got a different outlook on life, don't you, Julia?"

Her head tilted to the right as she ran one hand through her long hair, which she'd left free that day. "Different? I don't know. I'm sure there are many others who see things the same way I do. I'm not so revolutionary."

"I get the feeling you're pretty religious?" I shook my head. I shouldn't have said a thing like that—religion was never a great thing to bring up with coworkers. "Ignore me, Julia. I don't know what's gotten into me. I have no right to pry into your personal life so much."

She laughed, a light and happy sound. "I'm not worried about answering anything you want to ask me. And the thing is, I'm not religious at all, but I do consider myself very spiritual. My beliefs run deep. And I believe we all go somewhere when our bodies no longer function. Grandma and Gramps are where they're supposed to be now. Wherever that is."

I was impressed again by her. "So, you find no reason to be sad when a loved one passes on then?"

"What is there to be sad about?" she asked me with a serious look on her face. "Are you sad when a baby is born?"

"No. But death isn't the same thing as birth." I had no idea why she was comparing the two.

"When a baby is born, it makes a transition from one plane to another. Do you think the spirits on the other plane mourn the loss?" She looked at me with wisdom in her eyes that went well beyond her years.

How could someone so young hold that much wisdom in them?

I had to be honest. "This is all a bit over my head. I'm not a spiritual man. Mother made us go to church when we were kids, but when I got old enough to do what I wanted, I didn't go anymore. I don't believe in reincarnation, which it sounds like you do. I do believe in heaven and hell, and I think my parents went to heaven, and I hope I'll see them there. But I do feel sad about losing them from time to time. I definitely miss them not being in my life any longer."

She seemed to be pondering something as she rocked back and forth, her arms crossing her body as if she was hugging herself. "Do you ever dream about them?"

"At first I didn't. And then one night, about a year after their deaths, I did. And now I dream about them from time to time." Pushing my hand through my hair, I thought about the last dream I'd had about them. They were both in it, and there were bright pink flowers everywhere. We were in the middle of a meadow. I had no idea where, but I felt happier than I'd ever been, and they were there with me.

"Some people believe that when the dead come to you in your dreams, they're visiting you. I dream about my grandparents all the time." She sighed and sat on one of the sofas, looking as if she was recalling something. "The night before I saw the job listing for WOLF, I had a dream, and both of them were in it. I was running in a field covered in pink flowers. They were waiting for me on the other side of that field. All of a sudden, there was a pack of wolves running along with me. The leader was big and had thick black fur and piercing blue eyes." She looked directly into my eyes. "Eyes like yours, actually."

I had no idea what to say to that. The girl was intuitive, that was for sure. But was she more than that? I had to admit it was a bit scary, but far more intriguing. "And when you saw me for the first time, did you recall that?"

She shook her head. "I just remembered that right now. Funny, huh?"

Or maybe just projecting.

"Guess so." I looked at the computer screen, at the numbers she didn't like for the afternoon news, and wondered what we could do to spice that program up.

Suddenly she was right there next to me. "How about this idea? We bring in local heroes each day and bring their story to life. For instance, a firefighter who saved a boy in a burning building; we can ask what happened to him just before he did the heroic deed. We bring on a different New York hero each afternoon, making it all about that one person. We'll make the afternoon news extra local."

She'd done it again.

Lights went off in my head and I was immediately excited about it. "I say you're one hell of a smart young woman. That's a great idea."

She nodded. "Good. I like it a lot too. And we can really do it in a way that's different than anything else out there."

"We should really work on this as soon as possible. But that can't be right now, because we've got two video conferences to do, and then it'll be the end of the workday." I had a great idea. "Can you come to my place after work tonight?"

Julia nodded. "I am at your disposal, boss."

I liked the way she thought. "Good to know. Then I'll take you to my penthouse once we're done with the conferences. We'll have some dinner, then you and I can map out a real plan for the big change in that program."

"I'm in." She looked happy and satisfied. "I'm glad you and I think alike. It makes this so much more fun."

"I'm glad you have great ideas. That makes things so much easier." I got up and went to grab my cell from the breast pocket of my jacket, which I'd hung up earlier. "Now tell me what you want for dinner and I'll have my chef make it."

"I'm easy. I'll eat anything, so don't make anything special for me. I usually just eat a salad most nights." She ran her hand over her flat stomach, and I recalled the tiny amount she'd eaten the other day at lunch. And I hadn't been able to get her to go eat after that first day either. She always claimed she packed her lunch.

What she didn't know was that I checked the fridge in her office to see if she had anything in it. And it was always empty. I'd get the girl to eat if it was the last thing I did.

My chef knew how to make exceptional food. It would take more willpower to turn down her food than it did to turn down greasy burgers or pizzas.

"I'll tell her what to cook for us then, since you don't want to." I tapped in a text to the chef, telling her I wanted lobster and some salad of her choice to go along with it. I let her know I had company coming and that I wanted one of her best meals. I also asked her to relay to the housekeeper to make the small dining room an intimate and lovely experience for my guest.

I was about to show Julia how the other half lived. And I was determined to introduce her to healthy foods that she wouldn't feel bad about eating. She was not going to be starving herself—not on my watch. But I knew better than to talk to her about it just yet. I'd ease her into eating better without her realizing it.

"Do you drink wine, Julia?" I thought I should ask before telling the chef which wine I wanted with the meal.

"I'm not opposed to it. But I'm not a drinker by any means. One glass is about all I ever drink." She pulled out a pad of paper and a pen from my desk drawer. "Ready to head to the conference room to get things started?"

I was ready to get at least one thing started, and that was Julia on the road to feeling good about her body.

CHAPTER NINE

Julia

S itting in the back of Artimus's town car, I couldn't help but feel an unwarranted amount of excitement. He sat on the other seat across from me, and something about being in such a small, enclosed space made me think back to the way I'd felt that first day I'd met him. It was just business that had him taking me to his penthouse on 5th Avenue, I kept reminding myself.

I'd never even dared to dream about getting to see the inside of something like a New York City penthouse. I'd never thought something this exciting could happen to me.

I ran my hand over the soft tan leather seats. "Artimus, is everything you own this luxurious?"

A sly smile pulled his lips up to one side. "A lot of it. But I must confess that one of the things I cherish most is something that didn't cost a dime."

He pulled something out of his pocket. Whatever this thing was that he cherished so much was something he kept with him. I found that interesting. "You keep it with you?"

"Since the day it was given to me." He held out his palm, showing me a small, ugly, clay figurine. Browns and purples had been mixed together in a ball, and in the middle of the ball there was what looked like a fingerprint. "Angela, my baby sister, made this for me when she was in kindergarten. It was the first Christmas present she gave to me. She was so proud of it and told me to keep it with me always because she made it with love and it was my good luck charm." He ran his thumb over the fingerprint. "That's her tiny thumbprint. She told me that if I ran my thumb over it, she'd lend me some of her luck when I needed it."

My heart skipped a beat. "That's one of the sweetest things I've ever heard. What a wonderful big brother you are. And it's obvious you love your younger sisters. That says a lot about a man."

To me, it meant he knew a lot about females. He wouldn't be the kind of man who put women on pedestals, expecting them to be beyond human, the way some men did. He would know that we got up looking like we'd been ravaged by lions as we slept. Our hair would be a mess, our makeup smeared if we dared to go to sleep without washing it off. Our breaths would be questionable, and our moods could be cranky. We were, after all, human. Just like men.

Just one more thing that made him perfect. For me, at least.

As much chemistry as I felt between us on occasion, I'd never caught him looking at me the way I sometimes looked at him. He wasn't only business with me—he treated me like a friend more than an employee—but I knew he and I had a work relationship and that was all.

The car pulled to a stop, and Artimus pocketed his good luck charm as the driver came around to open the door. I slid out first, and Artimus came out right behind me. His hand touched the small of my back, sending sparks all through me. "I've got a surprise for you, Julia."

"You do?" I shivered and hoped he hadn't felt it. My stomach was tight and wet heat pooled between my legs.

If his hand on my back can make this happen, then how would I react to his hands all over my body?

Every day I spent with him made me more certain that I was meant to be with him. No one had ever brought out the things he brought out in me. But he was much older than me, and came from a different world. Plus, there was that nagging part of me that always reminded me that he could have any woman he wanted. He'd never want me. Not the way I'd want him to.

When we got up to his apartment, I pretty much lost any coolness I had in me. My mouth gaped as I looked at the lavish room we'd walked into. The foyer alone was remarkable, with paintings hanging on the three walls. "Is that a Monet?"

"It is." His hand still on the small of my back, he steered me to the left, and we went through a living area. It looked very formal, with expensive furniture that looked beautiful but also looked like it'd never been used. "The dining room I've asked my chef to serve dinner in is this way."

The next room had a bar in it. It was fully stocked, making me think he'd had many parties there. "Do you entertain much?"

"The boys and I play poker once a week. Other than that, no." His hand left my body, and I felt compelled to grab his hand to keep the physical contact going.

I didn't do that though. Holding my boss's hand wouldn't be appropriate at all.

He opened a door and there was the dining room. Once again, my mouth fell open as I looked around. A delicate chandelier hung over the table for two, and the round table had a white linen tablecloth draped over it. In the middle was a bouquet of white roses surrounded with green foliage, contrasting with all the white in the room.

Artimus pulled out a chair for me. "Have a seat, Julia." He chuckled as I sat down. "You look a little stunned."

"Well, this place looks like a five-star restaurant. I've never seen anything like this. It's kind of blowing my mind." The chairs were plush, with white fluffy seats that made it feel like I was sitting on a cloud.

He took the seat across from me, a delighted smile on his face. "Glad I could blow your mind."

Oh, the ways he could blow my mind.

My thoughts were broken by the entrance of a tall, slender, blonde woman. She looked to be in her mid- to late thirties. Much closer to Artimus's age than I was. And she was smiling at him as she pushed a cart into the room. "Hi there."

Artimus introduced us, "Tara, this is my new assistant, Julia Bengal."

"Nice to meet you, Julia," Tara said with a smile.

"You too, Tara." I felt odd all of a sudden, like he and she were old friends and I was an outsider.

I'd never felt that way at the station. I supposed it was because Artimus hadn't known any of those people much longer than he'd known me. But here, in his house, I could see the much more relaxed version of the man I worked for. And he was completely at ease with this woman. And I didn't like that much.

She placed a couple of wine glasses in front of us, then filled them with white wine. "I've made a three-course meal for you two this evening. We'll start with the amuse bouche." I must've looked lost, as she clarified what those words meant. "That's a fancy French way of saying flavorful bites. And I've made vichyssoise, which is made up of creamy potatoes and fresh leeks to start you off." She placed a small bowl in front of me, then put one in front of Artimus.

The portion size was so small, it boggled my mind. It was actually perfect for me, since I kept my carbs as low as I possibly could. Artimus took a bite with the equally tiny spoon it had been served with. "Delicious as always, Tara."

She was pleased with his praise. Her hand went to rest on top of his broad shoulder. "The lobster is coming up, and that will be followed by a desert. Be back in a few minutes."

"Thanks, Tara." His words were spoken to her, but his eyes were on me. "What do you think of it, Julia?"

I hadn't taken a bite yet. I hadn't eaten potatoes in years. But I wasn't about to be rude, so I dipped the spoon in and put the food in my mouth. Flavor virtually exploded in my mouth, and all I could do was moan with how good it was. "So good," I gasped. I didn't want to look like a glutton, but I wanted to devour that soup.

Artimus nodded. "Good. I like to see you enjoying your meals."

"It'd be impossible not to enjoy this. It's beyond compare to anything I've ever eaten." I ate the rest without saying a word, and then I took a sip of the wine, which was also delicious. "Wow, this is the best wine I've ever had, Artimus."

"Glad you like it. I've instructed Tara to open two bottles of the 2007 Domaine de la Romanée-Conti Montrachet. I thought you might like it." He sipped his and looked at me over the rim of the glass.

I wasn't sure if I was simply seeing what I wanted to see, or if he was actually giving me fuck-me eyes. Tara came in with the main dish, the lobster in crab sauce, which was also so good that I ate every last bite. I couldn't help myself. Lastly, she served us tiny raspberry sorbets that cleansed our palates.

Although everything was served in small proportions, I felt full. And that was something I hadn't felt in a while. Artimus grabbed the bottle of wine and both of our glasses. "Shall we retreat to the den?"

With a nod, I got up and followed him through room after room until we arrived in one that smelled of leather and musk, and a whole lot of Artimus Wolfe.

A fire burned in a fireplace, and the setting couldn't have been more romantic. The last thing I needed right then was for a romantic ambience to go along with the totally unprofessional, romantic feelings I was having for my boss. I looked around at all the deep chocolate furnishings that were partially obscured by the dim light. Tara came in behind us, the other bottle of wine in her hand, and she turned the lights up before going to place it on the coffee table. "Here you go, Artimus. I'll be in the kitchen if you want me."

"Thank you, Tara. You're a doll." He sat down and looked right at her, sitting in a big chair that seemed to be only his. "I'll call you if I need you."

She left us, leaving the door open behind her. I looked at him and felt I had to ask him a question, "Artimus, did you and Tara ever date?"

He shook his head before answering, "No. I've never dated anyone who works for me."

My heart crashed.

Never?

I knew what that meant and wasn't happy about it. But with so many good things happening in my life, I wasn't about to tempt fate by asking for any more than what I'd been given. I already had a great job working under a great boss, with terrific coworkers, to boot. Who could ask for more than that?

After planning out the new format for the afternoon news, we found that time had gotten away from us. It was eleven o'clock already, and I'd consumed more alcohol than I probably ever had, since the wine was so delicious. "Oh, Artimus. Look at the time. I should go."

I got up and he did too. But he didn't walk me out. Instead, he took both of my hands in his, standing in front of me. "Stay the night. My driver will take you home early in the morning so you can get dressed for work, and then he'll take you to work too. I'll drive myself to work tomorrow. It's late, and I've got plenty of bedrooms for you to choose from."

My eyes were locked on our clasped hands. My lips were numb from the alcohol, and my body was tired. A nice hot bath before hitting a comfy bed sounded like heaven to me. "Thank you, Artimus. I am tired."

He let go of one hand but still held the other as he led me to the hallway where the bedrooms were. He stopped at the first door. "This is my room. Would you like to stay in the one across the hallway?"

When he opened that door, I found a big bed that looked incredibly soft. "I didn't bring anything to sleep in," I said, trying not to blush.

"I'll grab you one of my T-shirts. Go take a bath and I'll leave it on your bed." He leaned forward, leaving a kiss on the top of my head. "See you tomorrow, Julia."

He closed the door and I just stood there. I was in my boss's house. I was about to wear his shirt to sleep in. And I knew I was going to have very realistic wet dreams, in a bed that belonged to Artimus Wolfe

CHAPTER TEN

Artimus

With Julia just across the hallway, my libido was in overdrive. I mean she was *right there*. Aside from the fact that she was my employee, I could tell she was a little on the tipsy side after our wine and work session. That made her vulnerable, and I'd never take advantage of a woman like that.

Damn my good moral fiber!

My cock was upset with me, straining against my pajama bottoms. I looked down at the tent it had made. "Stop it. You know I'm not that kind of man."

It pulsed at me, just to antagonize me, I was sure.

Looking at the bottle of water on my nightstand, I thought about Julia and thought maybe I should take her a bottle of water too. She had no idea where to get one, and it would be rude of me not to make sure she had access to anything she needed.

Wouldn't it?

Going to the small fridge in my bedroom, I took a bottle out and proceeded to the door. But my erection was still going strong, and that wouldn't be a very nice thing for her to see. So I went to the closet to get my robe, but as I stood in front of that door, I knew I wasn't going over there just to give her the water then leave. And that wasn't a good idea.

Going back to the fridge, I put the bottle back inside and went to get into my bed. Pulling the blanket up, I lay there, staring at the ceiling.

I wondered how long a person should wait before asking someone out who worked for them. *A week, a month, a year?*

Shaking my head to try to rid my mind of that thought, I switched to wondering how it would play out, dating someone who you also worked with. Everything would be great, until things fell apart and you'd be stuck seeing them at work every day.

I would've bet a million bucks that that would be as awkward as it got.

Had I made a mistake by hiring a woman I knew I was attracted to? Had I doomed myself to eternal sexual frustration because I'd listened to Ashton when he told me it wouldn't be fair not to give Julia the job? Would the feelings I had for Julia ever stop growing? Would they eventually die if I ignored them?

I had so many questions, and no one to ask them to.

One thing I did know was that there was no harm in having a little me-time, with that woman starring in my fantasy.

So, I did what any red-blooded American man would do. I took a hold of the situation. The situation being my throbbing cock.

Closing my eyes, I ran my hand up and down the length, pretending it was Julie who held me in a firm grip instead. We were sitting in the back of my car, the tinted windows hiding us from onlookers.

"I want you, Artimus," she murmured as her lips grazed my neck. Her hand moved fluidly around my dick.

With one forceful push, I had her on her back. Taking hold of her blouse, I pulled it apart, making buttons fly everywhere. Her tits heaved as she breathed heavily.

I pulled a knife out of my pocket and cut the front of her bra to set her big tits free. Grabbing them, I squeezed until she whimpered.

Then I bent down and took one in my mouth, licking that nipple until it was so hard it could cut glass. I sucked on it hard and long, making her cry out in ecstasy.

Her body was taut and tight as I ran my hands all over it, pulling her skirt down as I feasted on her delicious flesh. Down I went, kissing every inch of her gorgeous body as I did. I kept moving, all the way until I got to her sweet spot.

Looking up at her, I found her eyes open as she watched me. Her cunt tasted so sweet, I couldn't get enough of it. Her pearl was swollen, and I couldn't resist a little nibble on it. The sounds she made only made me eat her more ravenously.

Julia begged me to fuck her. Fuck her as hard as I could.

But she'd have to wait for that, because I wanted to taste her cum before I gave her my hard cock. Forcing my tongue into her tight hole, I fucked her with it until she clenched around my tongue and filled my mouth with her juices.

Drinking her in, I wanted to feel her mouth on me too. Pulling my face away from her dripping pussy, I looked at her. "On your knees."

Even though she panted from the orgasm she'd just had, she hurried to get on her knees in front of me. She looked longingly at my erection. "You want me to suck you?" Her dark eyes ran up to meet mine.

"You know what I want. Do it." I took her head in my hands and pulled her to take my cock into her mouth.

The wetness inside of her mouth lubricated my cock as I pulled her head back and forth, taking control and making her go as fast or as slow as I wanted her to. Her tongue ran up and down the underside of my dick as she deepthroated me.

"You like that, don't you, baby. You like my big dick going down your throat, don't you?"

Her moan told me that she did like it. And who wouldn't?

I spurted my load down her throat, and she drank it all. I let her head go, and she pulled back, wiping a few drops of my cum off her mouth with the back of her hand as she looked at me with fire in her eyes.

Huffing and puffing, I leaned back on the seat as she smiled at me sexily. Her eyes on me, she started pulling the remainder of her clothes off before getting on all fours and presenting her bare ass to me.

My cock sprang back to life as I looked at her round ass. I got off the seat to get on my knees behind her. Her ass begged to be spanked, and I gave her three nice smacks before shoving my erection in between her soaked walls.

She groaned with relief as I filled her pussy with my fat cock. "Yes, Artimus. Fuck me."

I pushed her shoulders down, pinning them to the floor so I could get deeper inside of her, burying my cock in her hot cunt.

"You like this fat cock thrusting into that sweet pussy, baby?" I pulled her hair as I slammed into her.

"Yes!" she screamed. "I love your fat cock, Artimus!"

"Mine is the only cock you get, baby. You understand me?" I thrust even harder into her tight hole.

"Yes, only you, Artimus," she panted and squirmed underneath me. "Only you. Forever."

Leaning over her, I growled into her ear, "You are mine. Only mine. Forever, Julia Wolfe."

My body tensed as an orgasm racked my body with an intensity I'd never felt before. I groaned as my seed filled her pulsing pussy.

Then she was there, in my bed with me, my arm around her sleeping body as we spooned together. I kissed the top of her shoulder as she made tiny snoring sounds. "Good night, baby. You're safe with me."

My eyes opened, clearing the vision from my head, and I looked up at the ceiling. My spent cock was still in my hand.

"What the hell was that all about, you crazy subconscious?" I'd spoken the words out loud. I had no idea where the last part of that fantasy had come from.

Julia Wolfe?

Was I really that invested in the woman?

Did a part of me really see her as a potential wife?

I shook my head before getting up to clean up the mess I'd made in my bed. Going to the shower to clean up, I turned on the water, then stepped into the tiled shower, which was big enough for six people if need be.

I had no idea why anyone would actually make a shower that damn big, but when people built things for the wealthy, they made everything bigger. Like the bathtub that was the size of a small swimming pool at my home in the Hamptons.

With that thought, I instantly imagined a naked Julia in that huge tub, the water bubbling all around her as the jets moved it around her body. She smiled at me, then wiggled her finger for me to come in and join her.

I got into the tub too, pulling her into my arms and kissing her. Our mouths fought for control but mine won, and she succumbed to me with a little moan. I lay back and put her on top of me, her cunt sliding down over my cock.

The water rocked us in its warm embrace. She sat up on top of me, putting on a show just for me as her hands moved through her hair and over her body, her boobs bouncing with each move she made.

I ran my hands up her tight stomach, then ground my thumb in circles around her clit. She gasped, her eyes going wide and then closing as she rode me until her body could take no more and she came all over my cock.

My eyes sprang open again, and I saw the remnants of cum washing down the drain. I'd come again in a matter of a few minutes. And that was only from fantasizing about her.

What would having sex with her in real life be like?

Maybe I was putting her up on some kind of pedestal. No one could be that great in bed.

Right?

I looked down to find my cock hard again. "This can't be real."

I had to be dreaming. I'd never gotten hard back-to-back like that.

Not that I wasn't an accomplished lover. I was. But I hadn't been able to get hard that quickly after an orgasm since I was a teen. Not since I was just beginning puberty and it was all so new and exciting to me.

After jacking off one more time to get rid of that hard-on, I got out of the shower, put new sheets on my bed, and climbed into it. I then tossed and turned for too long, having a hard time falling asleep knowing that the woman of my dreams lay just across the hallway from me.

I had no idea what the right thing to do was. All I did know was that I needed to get this under control, no matter what.

Now that I'd broken the seal, so to speak, I had a horrible feeling that my cock would be taking over, leaving my brain in the dust. And that was never a good idea.

Nothing good could come from leading with your sexual organs instead of rational thought.

My eyes finally felt heavy, and sleep finally came to take me into its arms. And yet I still found Julia waiting for me. Her arms wide open, her body bare, and her face just as beautiful as ever as she beckoned me to come to her.

I moved with a steady pace, then took her in my arms, and she felt like she'd been there forever. She felt like I wanted to keep her there forever. And the name, Julia Wolfe, just kept echoing around us, surrounding us like a thick blanket, protecting us both from the cold.

CHAPTER ELEVEN

Julia

The wine knocked me out as soon as my body hit the bed, thankfully. Artimus was the only thing on my mind as I bathed that night. I thought of a million reasons why I needed to go to his bedroom, but I was lucky enough that all the wine I'd drunk made me too tired to think of any excuse that stuck. It kept my ass in my own bed, leaving the boss alone for the night.

I'd have been humiliated if I'd woken up in his bed.

Getting up super early so I could get back to my apartment to get ready for the workday, I called Artimus's driver, telling him I was ready to be picked up.

As I walked out of the building, I found dawn had come, and it was light enough outside for me to see my surroundings. To my astonishment, I saw Price Stone sitting in his car just across the street from the building Artimus lived in.

To make things even more astonishing, he stayed long enough to wave at me before taking off with a frown on his face.

Is he stalking me?

If he was, he didn't seem to even be trying to hide what he was doing anymore. And that was scary.

I got into the backseat of the car and took my cell out of my purse, debating whether or not to call the jackass and bitch him out.

In the end, I decided not to engage with him. I'd leave him thinking that I didn't care what he was doing. Maybe that would finally show him that I wasn't going to give him any of my attention. Maybe then he'd move on.

I'd come to the conclusion that Price Stone had never been told *no* before. That had to be the reason he was being so tenacious—he liked getting his way, and I wasn't letting him.

The driver waited outside of my apartment building while I got ready, so I hurried, thankful that Bethey was still asleep and out of my way. Sharing one bathroom wasn't always easy.

Going back down to the car, I found Price sitting in his own vehicle just across the street again. He waved once more, and I shot the finger at him.

I knew I shouldn't have done that. It was just giving him attention, after all. But I couldn't stand him thinking he was getting away with anything.

Once again, I held my cell phone in my hands, contemplating calling him and telling him he had to back off or I was going to have to go to the authorities to make him stop.

But as I sat there in the back of the car, thinking about that, I knew no one would help me. Except for that one time, the time I didn't even report to the police, Price hadn't hurt me at all. He'd just asked me for another chance and told me how sorry he was.

Who would go out of their way to help me when I'd missed the opportunity to turn him in when he'd first hit me?

Getting to the office, I went inside, looking over my shoulder to see if Price's car was anywhere to be seen. I didn't see anything, so I went inside and up to my office.

How could Price think he could just keep bothering me like this? I had told him a million times that things were over between us, forever. I didn't even want to be the man's friend. And yet, he still had the audacity to follow me around.

Did he know I'd spent the night with my boss? Had he followed the car when Artimus and I left the station last night to go to his place? And if he had, had he gone so far as to go inside and try to find out which apartment was Artimus's?

My mind ran away with me as I went up the long elevator ride to the top floor. On one hand, I wasn't afraid of Price at all. On the other, there was a nagging worry that he might do something crazy.

As if following me around the city wasn't crazy enough already, I scoffed to myself. But what would I do if he took things even further?

What if he hit me again? Would I call the police? Or would I walk away, the way I had last time, and not report a thing to anyone at all?

I hadn't told a single soul what he'd done to me. Shame filled me about that now.

I should've told at least one other person about that incident, when the bruises were still fresh for them to see.

Now he could say I was lying, and I wouldn't have even one person to back me up on what my accusations were.

I'd made a big mistake, I was realizing, but I had no idea how to rectify it at all.

When I got to the top of the building and stepped off the elevator, I saw Brady scrubbing away at the seats in the lobby. "Good morning, Brady. Is the boss in yet?"

"Not yet, Julia." He stopped his incessant cleaning to point down the hall, the blue surgical gloves on his hands making them stand out. "Someone sent bagels and donuts to all of us up here on the top floor this morning. If you're interested, it's all in the first conference room. I've left that door open, so everyone can go in and grab something if they want."

With a nod, I asked, "Have you grabbed anything for yourself?"

"Oh, not me," He shook his head as he gave me a serious look. "I only eat what I make myself. One never knows what someone else might be doing to the food, after all. But you go ahead and enjoy. You eat out all the time. Your stomach is practically the same as a stray dog's by now."

With no idea how to take that, I decided to forgo the food and went straight to my office. Brady, being a major germaphobe, didn't intend to say rude things like that, but from time to time some managed to come out. I couldn't let it get to me.

Opening the laptop on top of my desk, I took a seat then set to work on checking out last night's ratings. My fingers drummed on the desktop as I looked at some satisfying numbers.

After a few minutes, the phone on my desk rang, which hadn't happened once since my first day. I answered it without having a clue as to who it was, which felt odd after having Caller ID on my phone forever. "Hello?"

"Julia Bengal, please," came a woman's voice.

"This is she," I answered, feeling a little odd about it for some reason.

"This is WOLF reception in the lobby. I've got Price Stone from *The New York Times* here to see you, Miss Bengal."

My breath caught in my throat.

Why is he here?

"He doesn't have an appointment," I finally managed to get out as I bit my pinky fingernail nervously. I did not want Price Stone up in my office at all.

"She says you haven't made an appointment, Mr. Stone. Would you like me to see if she has time available to see you soon?" she asked Price.

"Please," I could hear him say. "It's very important that I see her this morning."

I had to wonder why that would be. He and I didn't have one thing to talk about.

"He'd like to make an appointment then, Miss Bengal," she informed me.

I had no idea what the hell to say to that. But finally, something came to me just as Artimus strolled through my door. "I'm not accepting any appointments this week. He'll have to call next week to see if I'm free. Bye." I hung up the phone as Artimus walked toward me.

He shook his head as he looked at me. "What was that about, Julia? You look a bit shaken."

"Someone wanted to make an appointment with me. It didn't seem right, so I made up an excuse, saying I'm busy all week. I didn't know what else to do." My hands were clasped in my lap, but I began to fist them with aggravation and a little bit of fear, too.

What the hell is Price thinking?

The phone in Artimus's office began to ring, and I jumped up to answer it, nearly sprinting from my office to his. I picked up the phone, feeling Artimus right behind me. "Artimus Wolfe's office, Julia speaking."

"Julia, it's me, Price. What the hell are you doing?" His words came out sounding tense, as if he were clenching his jaw.

I couldn't talk to him the way I wanted to with Artimus standing so close. "How can I help you today, sir?"

"Oh, I get it. Playing it up for the boss man. Sure, I can go along with that, baby. I'd like to interview him for the *New York Times*. What do you say? Think you can hook me up?" I could feel my body go rigid at what appeared to be his stupendous idea for infiltrating my job. "And I've already sent a peace offering, too. Did you get the donuts and bagels I had sent to you guys this morning?"

So he was the one who'd sent the food. I was sure glad I hadn't had any of it. "No," came my stoic response. It took quite a bit to make that one word come out sounding so calm. I wanted to scream it, along with a string of curse words that would've made sailors blush.

"No, huh?" He was quiet for a moment. "Maybe I should talk directly to him then, since you're being difficult. How many times do I have to say I'm sorry before you forgive me for one drunken mistake, baby?"

I hated that he still called me baby. I hated that he'd come to the place I worked and planned on using Artimus to get to me. "Don't."

"Don't what? Don't care about you?" Price just couldn't seem to stop himself, as he went on, "I can't stop doing that, and you know that. Look, I know I was your first real boyfriend. You just don't know how couples work. People make mistakes, and then they say they're sorry, and then you forgive them and move on with the relationship. It's what grownups do, baby. I was drunk. You shouldn't hold the sober me accountable for what the drunk me did. Hell, I don't even remember doing any of what you told me I did the next day."

"Well, I'm sorry that you don't understand." I started thinking about my job and what that meant. I couldn't just say that Artimus couldn't do the interview without asking him about it. "Let me ask my boss, and I'll get back to you about that."

"Great. You've got my number. I look forward to hearing your pretty voice on my cell again. I've missed you like you can't understand, baby."

I hated the man. "Bye."

Artimus looked at me with a curious expression. "Ask me what?"

Placing the phone back on his desk, I took a deep breath so the anger I felt wouldn't come through in my words. "Price Stone from *The New York Times* would like to interview you."

Artimus put one hand into his pocket while the other held his chin. "Do you know if he's any good?"

He's no good at all. He's a man who hits women!

But as a writer, he was excellent. I couldn't say anything other than that. "He's good at his job, sir."

Artimus furrowed his brow. "Sir? I don't think that's necessary, Julia. Just Artimus is fine. Let's not go backward. And if he's good and you can vouch for that, then I'm fine with doing the interview. It might get us even more viewers, right?"

I knew that it would. So even though I didn't want him to do the interview with Price, I had to say, "It should."

But I don't want to be around the asshole.

Artimus took his seat behind his desk. Pulling open the top drawer, he looked over the large calendar inside. "Set it up for a week from this Friday. At the penthouse. And I want you to be there too."

I'd known he would. "Of course."

And now I have to see that fucking ass-wipe again and try to hide everything from Artimus. Shit!

CHAPTER TWELVE

Artimus

With the interview for the *New York Times* set up, the newspaper decided that they also wanted to do a photoshoot with me, so Julia and I were headed to Bergdorf Goodman to get something to wear.

We sat in the back of my car. I'd been noticing that something wasn't right with her. "You okay?"

She stared out the window, looking at nothing in particular. "Huh?" It wasn't like her to be so spacey.

"Are you okay, Julia?" I reached out to run my hand over her shoulder. "You haven't exactly been yourself these last few days. Is everything okay?"

"Yeah, sure." She looked at me with a smile on her face. But it was forced, I could tell that much.

There had to be something bothering her. "You can tell me anything. I want you to know that." I meant it, too. Our friendship was growing all the time. Even with her being out of sorts, she and I grew closer with each passing day.

My driver stopped at our destination and Julia took the opportunity to avoid having to explain anything to me. "Here we are, Artimus."

I let it go for the time being. But I was set on getting her head out of the fog it had been in. On a good note, I did have her eating more than she was when she first started her job. I called out for lunch and had it delivered every day. The key was small portions of delectable food, and she'd eat it all up.

As soon as we got inside and the salesladies descended upon us, I made sure she knew she was getting a new outfit too. "I'm here for something dressy yet casual, and I want her in something sophisticated and timeless."

Julia looked at me with a frown. "We're here to get you something, Artimus. Not me."

I cocked my head to the side as I shoved my hands into my pockets. "Who knows. They might want a picture of both of us both. You know, the woman behind the man."

"Oh, is this your wife, sir?" one of the salesladies asked.

Julia was quick to reply, "No. I'm just his assistant." She cut her eyes at me. "I don't know why he'd say such a thing."

"Because you are the woman behind me. I would be lost without you. So, come on, and let's get our clothes picked out for this photo shoot." I grabbed her hand, pulling her along with me.

Reluctantly, she came along, but I could tell she was going to argue about everything along the way. "This is crazy," she leaned in to whisper. "And I can't afford a damn thing in this store."

"You don't have to worry about that. We'll write it down as a business expense." A thought came to me all of a sudden. "I'm opening an account for you here. I want to see you in something new and expensive each day."

She didn't look pleased at all, and her tone was serious. "No way."

I should've expected that reaction, but hadn't. So I told her a little white lie. "It's on WOLF, Julia. You need to look the part of my assistant. And I know you don't have the funds for that. As a business account, the station can write off all the purchases you make."

She slowed down, thinking for a moment. "We do have those

meetings with the FCC in a few weeks. I probably should dress a bit savvier than I normally do." She looked at me with her lips pulled to one side, making little wrinkles appear around her mouth. "Okay, I'll accept a company account."

"Good. You can have a stylist help you out too. Perhaps you could take this weekend to get yourself a number of items to add to your wardrobe. Make a day out of it. Have some fun." I'd been wondering if Julia was having any fun at all. She'd been working so hard, spreading herself so thin for me. I didn't want to dominate all her time.

"Bethey would love to help me shop." She nodded. "I'll do that, then."

Happy to hear she'd have someone to shop with, I decided to add a bit to her weekly pay. It would mean I'd have to give the same bonuses to the rest of the employees, but I was ready to do that. I was ready to do anything that would get that beautiful smile back on her face.

"No better weekend to do that than this upcoming one. Friday's paychecks have the bonuses in them. So you'll have more than enough extra money to help you have a great weekend." I smiled, patting myself on the back for being so clever.

The saleslady stopped and pointed at the menswear section. "Randolph will help you, sir."

"Okay. I want Julia to come with me though. I need her advice on what I pick out today." I pulled her along with me, and the saleslady seemed a bit put out, probably worrying she was about to lose the commission that would go along with helping Julia. "Not to worry. We'll have Randolph call you when we're done here."

A smile replaced the anguished expression she'd worn. "Tell him to call Phoebe, please."

Julia smiled reassuringly at her. "We will, Phoebe. And I'll ask for you when I come back on Saturday if you're working that day."

The lady was over the moon now. "Oh, I will be working on Saturday. From nine in the morning to seven in the evening. Please do ask for me. And your name is?"

"Julia Bengal." She waved at the woman. "See you in a bit."

"I'll get some things together for you in the meantime to speed things up for you, Julia." And with that, the woman left with a skip in her step as she saw dollar signs in her future.

Randolph showed up with a tape measure laid across his neck. "Hi. Are you looking for something in particular?"

Julia stepped right up, taking over the way she was so good at. "He's going to need to look dressed up and professional, but in a casual way. I like him in dark blues, and deep browns accent his hair well. So, let's start looking at those color wheels and see where that takes us."

As we followed the salesman, I nudged her with my shoulder. "I like the color red on you, just so you know."

Her cheeks went red as she tugged her hand out of mine. "You're so silly."

I wasn't trying to be silly at all. I was trying to move things forward with her. Her mood had put a halt to most of the plans I'd decided on for how to move our working relationship to a romantic one.

After that crazy, hot night of her at the center of my fantasies and dreams, I'd decided to start laying the groundwork for me and her to start something.

Of course, there was the off chance that we might not last forever—even though that word seemed to be as much a part of my fantasies as Julia herself—but that was a chance I was willing to take.

While Randolph picked out some outfits, I took a seat and made her take one too. "Sit. Let him do all the legwork."

She sat down in the chair next to mine. "You're right. I should let him do his job." She tapped her fingers on the rails as she sat back. Her body looked relaxed, but the tapping nails told me something was on her mind.

Something that had been on her mind for the last few days and now was as good a time as any to get into it. "While we're waiting, I'd like to get to the bottom of this mood you've been in."

Her nails stopped tapping as she looked at them, then me. "Why do you think I've been in a mood?"

My eyes rolled of their own volition. "Really, Julia?"

She looked down at the floor. "You notice too much."

I had to laugh at that. "You and I spend too much time together for me not to. And maybe I could help you out of this funk if you just tell me what put you in it in the first place."

Her eyes held mine for a very long time, and I knew she was considering whether or not she should let me in on what was going on. But then Randolph showed up with an armload of things for me to try on. "Here you go, sir. Let me show you to the dressing room over here."

Julia got up and followed along, taking a seat outside of the dressing room. "Make sure you come out and show me each outfit, Artimus. I want you to look fantastic for this shoot."

So I had to drop the conversation right there. For the next two hours, I played model for her as she nitpicked everything that Randolph had picked out for me.

In the end, she mixed up a shirt he'd chosen and found a pair of slacks she picked out herself, and then added a pair of shoes he said would work well with the ensemble.

I finally had my clothes picked out, and we went to get her something too. I'd never tried on so many damn clothes in my life and vowed I would never shop for myself with her again.

I had wanted to let my stylist pick something out and send it to me, but Julia wasn't having any of that. She wanted me to be as close to perfect as possible for this interview. She even went so far as to make up some questions for me to answer and gave me several mock interviews.

With her as my coach, I didn't think failure was an option.

As we looked through the clothes her saleslady had picked out, I found Julia wasn't nearly as picky about her own clothes as she'd been with mine.

Her exact words were, "The red dress, the black heels, the black pearl necklace. Wrap that up, and we'll be ready to go."

"Add some matching pearl earrings," I added. "And a purse, too—something nice and expensive. Like that black Givenchy over there. That one will do."

"Artimus, that's too much," Julia argued. "I've got a black purse already and some earrings too."

I could only shake my head. "No. I want it all to match." I looked at the saleslady. "If you have a bracelet that'll match, add that too."

Julia crossed her arms over her chest. "Artimus!"

"It's on the station and is a tax write-off, Julia. Now let me do what I have to in order to keep our tax debt down." I was particularly proud of coming up with that excuse as a reason to buy her things.

The fact was that it made me happy to buy her stuff. It made me happy to order things that I knew she'd eat. The expense was nothing compared to the joy I felt when I was able to provide anything for her.

I knew she loved everything she'd gotten that day. I had even overheard her and the saleslady talking about how gorgeous everything was and how happy Julia was with everything. And they were already talking about what they'd be looking at on Saturday.

So Julia could balk all she wanted. I knew our little shopping trip had improved her bad mood. If I hadn't already known as we left the cash register, I would have known a few minutes later when we got into the car. As my driver was putting the purchases in the trunk, she reached across and hugged me.

Her smile was bright when she let me go. "Thank you, boss. You've brightened my day."

The only thing that would've made that moment better was if I'd gotten to kiss her. But that would have to wait. The groundwork had to be laid out first.

CHAPTER THIRTEEN

Julia

The day of the photo shoot had arrived. Artimus was taken away, much to his dismay, and I was told to stay in a waiting room. Flipping through social media on my cell, I sat in an uncomfortable chair with my ankles crossed.

I'd donned a Fendi cold-shoulder knit top in blue and green with thin horizontal stripes. It was only one of the items I'd picked up on my weekend shopping trip to Bergdorf Goodman. As unsure as I'd felt when Artimus had first suggested the trip, it hadn't been a hardship at all to pick out so many lovely items.

With Bethey there to help me put money out of my mind, I'd let myself go and bought what I wanted without worrying about how I would ever pay the bill. Since WOLF was taking care of it all, I had nothing to worry about.

The shirt I wore cost just under a thousand dollars, making it something I never would've even looked at on my own. The whip-stitch black leather pencil skirt I'd bought as a staple of my new wardrobe cost over three thousand dollars. Another item I would never have considered if I had to pay that price myself. But Bethey and the saleslady had both told me that the skirt would outlast me. It was a piece that would go with almost anything, and I would come to depend on that skirt as one of my go-to pieces of clothing.

When you added the knee-high runway mesh boots in black, also made by Fendi, my outfit was worth around five thousand dollars—and it felt that way too. I exuded confidence in my new clothes. I had never imagined that wearing expensive clothing would affect me the way it had.

The sound of the door opening had me looking up to see who it was. "No," came my quick response as I saw the familiar figure.

Price Stone ignored me as he came in, closing the door behind him. The room had no windows, and there was only one door to get in or out of there, and he stood right in front of it, looking me up and down.

He looked at me with an expression of such disgust that I found it genuinely disorienting. I didn't understand that look at all. I'd never looked better, in my opinion. WOLF had also paid for me to get my hair cut and styled, and I now wore it in long layers that felt like silk as they flowed around my face, framing it in a way it never had before.

Putting my cell away in my purse, I had to let him know one thing. "I don't want you in here, Price."

"So." He continued to look me over then gestured to me with one long dip of his hand. "What the hell is this, Julia? Designer clothes that cost more than you could ever afford?" He shook his head. "I never pegged you as a gold digger. But here you are, apparently digging away at Artimus Wolfe's riches."

Feeling incensed, I narrowed my eyes at the shithead. "He didn't pay for these things. It's for the station. WOLF expects me to look a certain way—I am the owner's assistant, after all. We have meetings and other things to attend where I'll need to be dressed just as well as those we're meeting with, Price." Another thought came to me, and I felt the need to add, "And I don't want you to tell my boss anything about our past relationship."

The glare he'd already been wearing only got worse, and fire seemed to be sparking behind his blue eyes. "First of all, I won't be answering any questions during our interview; he will. And second, there are more than a few people who know about us, baby. Who's to say someone else here at the *New York Times* won't tell him about you and me?"

That thought hadn't occurred to me. But I doubted anyone would bother to tell Artimus Wolfe something like that about his assistant. It seemed trivial, and I couldn't imagine it coming up. "I'm not worried about that. I am worried about you messing things up for me though."

Price shifted his weight, making me think he didn't to want to walk away from blocking the door, no matter how uncomfortable it was for him to just stand there. "What things are there for me to mess up? You mean me messing up your chance at getting the man to fuck you, Julia?"

Now I was royally pissed. "You know better than that, Price. You know how I feel about sex. How dare you say a thing like that to me?"

A smirk formed on his lips. "You are nothing but a little fucking cock-tease, Julia. You led me around by the fucking nose for six months, making out with me then leaving me with blue balls, using your idiotic notion of only ever being with one man as your excuse."

I had no idea how he could call my ideals an excuse. "Do you hear yourself? Or do you just talk without listening to a thing you say? I was only ever upfront with you, and I've lived my whole life with that plan and have no reason to change my mind. What makes you think I teased you? What makes you think I used anything as an excuse not to have sex with you? I told you how I felt. I told you about how I wasn't going to have sex with you. You're the one who said that was okay and that you still wanted to see me."

"I thought that one day you would get over that shit and grow the fuck up." He slammed his fist into the side of his leg. "You have no idea how fucking frustrating you can be, do you?"

I looked at his fist as he clenched it at his side. He wanted to take that fist and slam me in the jaw with it, the way he had before. Only he'd always blamed the alcohol for that night. Now he was stone-cold sober.

Would he actually hit me again while sober? Here?

The first thing I thought about was getting the hell out of that room. "I've got to go." I got up and found his hands on my shoulders. "Price, let me go," I tried to keep my tone stern and unshakeable, but I had to admit there was an edge of fear to it, and I knew he could hear that as well.

His blue eyes were seething with anger. "What makes you think that you're any better than anyone else, you bitch?"

Bitch?

No one called me that. I wasn't about to let him get away with it either. "Listen to me, Price Stone. I am not a bitch. I do not think I'm better than anyone. I just have a set of rules I live my life by, and you have no right to call me names just because you don't agree with them. I expect anyone who wants to be involved with me to accept that or move the fuck on. I didn't beg you to be with me; you chose to be with me. I didn't make you any false promises the way you did me."

Shock replaced his angry expression, and his hold on me loosened. "What kind of false promises did I make to you, Julia?"

His words ruminated in my brain, so I repeated them, "Julia, I don't want more than you're willing to give. I only want to be in your life."

His head dropped. "I do remember saying that to you."

Moving his hands off me, I felt like I'd brought him back to the man he usually was, instead of the forceful jackass he could become. Price Stone wasn't all bad. When he was good, he was very good. When he was bad, he was very bad. And that bad part of him was just more than I cared to take.

I decided to remind him of how good he could be. "Price, you're really a nice man, most of the time. I think the sexual frustration may have made you hit me that night. You should forget about me and move on. Be with someone who has the same ideals as you and then the monster you can become most likely won't come out again."

I hadn't meant to provoke the man at all, but the fire in his eyes told me that I had done just that. "I am not a monster. If you want to know what I think, I think that you're the one who's a monster, Julia. You little prick tease."

No one had ever called me so many names in my life. This man had hit me and called me names. All I wanted was to get away from him, but he didn't seem to care about what I wanted. I felt like he was some kind of parasite, intent on sucking me dry for some unknown reason.

Could me not having sex with him really have caused all this? Or was there more to it?

All I knew for sure was that I wanted to get out of that room and the hell away from him. "I'm done with this." I turned to leave once more, heading toward the door.

In a swift movement, I found him once again grabbing me by the shoulders before pinning me to the wall. His hot breath flowed over my face, his lips mere centimeters from mine as he pressed his forehead against mine. "No, you're not done with this." His body held me against the wall while he moved one hand up to cup my face in his palm. "Julia, I am sorry, baby. I really am. I care so damn much about you. It makes me do things I normally wouldn't."

I didn't care what he said. I knew he was capable of controlling himself. "Things like hitting me and then stalking me when you didn't get your way?"

"Please stop talking about that." His lips grazed my cheek. "Let's just put this behind us, baby. I just want to get back to where we were before you said I hit you."

His audacity stupefied me. "I didn't just *say* that you hit me, Price. When you came to my apartment the next day, I showed you the bruise on my cheek that I had to hide with makeup. I showed you the five bruises your fingers left on each of my arms as you gripped me so tightly when I tried to leave your place."

Once again, he used the same excuse I'd heard way too many times already. "I don't remember doing any of that, baby. I really don't. All I do recall is waking up on my living room floor with a huge knot on my head, and you gone."

"I'm not rehashing this with you anymore, Price." I huffed with anger and frustration, his body pressing mine against the wall beginning to feel suffocating. "Now let me go."

His hand ran down my skirt before hiking it up a little. "I could fuck you right here, baby. I could rid you of that precious gift you have and end all of that nonsense for you. Maybe then you'd see fit to forgive me and give me another chance."

I could feel his cock pressing against me as it thumped in his pants at the evil thoughts he was having. He and I were all alone in the room. Price was stronger than me. He really could do everything he said, and unless someone walked in to help me, I wouldn't be able to stop him.

So, I had to make what I said sound real convincing, or something might go very wrong for me. Gathering every ounce of courage I had, I made my tone stern and serious. "Price Stone, if you don't let me go within three seconds, I will bring my knee up and fuck up the rest of your day."

He pulled his head back to look into my eyes, and I made sure mine told him that I was being entirely serious. I would knee him in the jewels if he didn't let me go.

Moving back, he let me go, looking tired and defeated. "I never wanted things to be this way, Julia. Not ever." And then he left me without saying another word.

Stumbling to a chair, I fell into the seat, fighting back the urge to cry. I had to stay strong. No matter how much he'd scared me, I had to act as if nothing had just happened, and least until I was in the privacy of my own home, where I could process what had just taken place.

This had to stop before something terrible happened.

CHAPTER FOURTEEN

Artimus

Sitting in Price Stone's office at the *New York Times*, I couldn't help but feel a little odd. The man sat there at his desk, acting as if he was in charge of the whole damn company. Which he wasn't. I had the distinct impression he was trying to out-alpha me for some reason.

We had already had a bit of an issue getting the interview off the ground in the first place, as he had been entirely unwilling to conduct the interview at my penthouse as I'd initially requested. That alone didn't leave me with the best impression of the guy, and it just kept getting worse by the second.

Julia sat next to me, fiddling with her cell as Price ran his finger over a sheet of paper, which I assumed had the questions that he'd be asking me written down. He cocked one blond eyebrow then looked at me. "Hmm, this is interesting, Artimus. It says here that you've never been married and that you're thirty-six years old. Is that right?"

"Yes, it is." I had no idea what the man was getting at or what my lack of wedding bells—or my age, for that matter—had to do with anything.

His lips pulled up to one side as he asked me another question. "Does that mean you're not entirely heterosexual then?"

Stunned, I sat there in disbelief. *Is this jackass kidding?* "I am entirely heterosexual, Stone. What are you trying to say? And why is that relevant to WOLF?"

With a shrug, he went on, "Men your age are usually either married or at least divorced. And most men your age have children. Any children no one knows about, Artimus?"

This guy wasn't turning out to be what I thought he was. I looked at Julia. "I thought you said he was good, Julia. Not some asshole with an agenda to ruin me."

Julia stopped messing with her cell to look at Price. "The remainder of the questions you ask will be aimed at getting to know Mr. Wolfe and his company," she tapped her nails on his desk, "I've heard you call him by his first name several times and I don't want to hear that again. He is Mr. Wolfe to you, Mr. Stone. One more irrelevant question and this interview is over." She held up the consent form to show him. "And I will shred this consent form, and you won't have one word you can write about Mr. Wolfe. Do you understand me, Mr. Stone?"

All he did was nod and look a bit pissed. But after that, the rest of the interview went fine. I had to admit that Julia had not only surprised me with the way she'd handled the situation, but had impressed me more than she already had in the past. And I'd already found her very impressive.

After the interview was over, she and I got into the back of my car, and the driver took us back to the office. Julia hadn't been herself the whole time we were in Price Stone's presence. I wondered if she felt about him the way I had. "That man was a wolf in sheep's clothing. What did you think of him, Julia?"

She nodded. "That's a good way of putting it. He gives off a bad vibe."

He did more than that. "He looks like some upright, great guy. I think it's the blond hair and blue eyes—they make him look trustworthy and charming, which I doubt he is. I can see right through that man. He's not what he seems to be."

"I agree." She looked out the window, seeming kind of melancholy. "But none of that matters. You don't ever have to deal with that man again. He's a thing of the past. Don't give the jerk a second thought."

I knew she was right. Why waste an ounce of time or energy on a man like Price Stone?

But I did want to say one more thing. "Julia, he acted like he was jealous, in my opinion. Like it was all some pissing contest to prove he was a better man than me. I can't figure out any other reason why he'd question my sexuality like that. Do you think he has a thing for you, and that's why he acted that way?"

She shook her head. "No. I think he's just an insecure asshole. Now, let's not talk about him anymore. He leaves a bad taste in my mouth."

She was right about that. He'd left a bad taste in mine too. So I moved on to other business. Not that it was really business so much as social, and step one in my plan to get Julia to see me in a romantic light. "Do you have any plans for Saturday night?"

"This Saturday night?" she asked as she pulled up the calendar on her phone.

"Yes, this one." My nerves began to kick in. I took a deep breath to calm them. *Please be free.*

Tapping the screen of her phone, she said, "I'm free." She looked at me. "Why do you ask?"

Please say yes. "I've been invited to a charity event. The invitation has a plus one, and I thought, since it's only a day away, that you might go to it with me." She looked like was on the fence, so I added, "I'd hate to have to try to get a date last minute. I hope you'll come with me and save me the problem of finding one."

It was the right approach—she was always ready to help someone who needed it. "In that case, I'll be happy to go with you. But I have no idea what I should wear to something like this. Do you?"

You'd look great in anything.

I didn't say that though. "I'll send something over for you to wear so you'll feel comfortable and will fit in with the crowd." I wanted to buy her something anyway. I loved looking at things and picturing her in them. It had become a hobby of mine, although I'd never meant for it to become one.

Julia rarely left my mind. I fell asleep thinking about her, dreamt about her, and even woke up thinking about her. Anytime I found myself without something to think about, there she was.

The event should have some dancing at it, and my arms already ached to hold her while we danced. It would be the first time I'd get to hold her the way I'd been dreaming to. If she could dance. "Julia, do you like to dance?"

She nodded. "I have no idea if I'm any good or not, but I give it my all."

"That's good to hear. There should be dancing at this event. I haven't cut a rug in a while."

One dark brow cocked. "Oh, you mean like dancing, dancing. Like with partners? Not dancing by yourself, right?"

"Yes, I mean the type of dancing where I lead, and you follow. That kind. Can you do that?" I crossed my fingers on the side of my leg, where she couldn't see what I was doing. It was childish and silly, but I couldn't help myself.

Her head bobbed. "It's been a long time, like probably since senior prom, since I danced that way. But I'm game if you are. I might step on your toes a little at first, so as long as you can handle that, we can give it a try."

I could handle her stepping on anything. As long as I got to hold her in my arms while she did it. "I think I can handle that."

"Do you think it'll be fun?" she asked, her hand sliding through her silky hair.

With her, everything is fun.

"We'll make sure it is." Taking my cell out, I pulled up the website of the charity to show her the webpage with all the information about the event. Holding my finger on the web address, I copied it and emailed it to her.

She looked at her phone as it dinged, and didn't say a word while she checked it over. "This does look cool. The Humane Society does such great things for animals. That's so nice that you donate to their cause."

If she thought that was nice, then she'd love what else I did for that cause. "My family has always been a big supporter. I even let the Humane Society foster some of their animals that are harder to place at my home in the Hamptons." I pulled up some pictures of the various animals who were guests at my home. "Stanley is the trainer I hired to take care of them and teach them how to behave before they're ready to be put up for adoption." I showed her a German shepherd that was a biter before Stanley got a hold of him. "Hans Gruber—his former name—is a success story. He was taken away from his owner, who had been using him as a fighting dog. When the police raided a dog fighting club, all of the animals were taken to the Humane Society."

Julia put her hand over her mouth, her expression one of horror. "That's horrible."

"I agree. I took Stanley to see all the dogs and told him to pick out any of them he thought he could rehabilitate into suitable pets. Out of all twelve of those poor dogs, he only picked one who he thought could overcome the torture he'd been through." I showed her the picture of the poor dog when we first saw him. "This is the way Hans looked before we got him."

A long sigh came out of her. "There's such sadness in his dark eyes. It kills me to think he once looked like that. The first picture you showed me made me think he'd never had a bad day in his whole life."

Nodding in agreement, I put my cell away. "That's the magic of Stanley. I'll take you out there to meet him and his rescued animals someday soon. I think you'd enjoy that."

"To the Hamptons?" she asked with wide eyes. "Wow."

Looking at Julia in her fine clothing, seeing the way she held herself, and knowing how quickly she had been able to sink into the part of a professional New York City woman, it was easy for me to forget that there was an innocent girl underneath all that. One who had very little experience with life in general, and yet no one would guess that unless they talked to her for a while.

Julia was a mixture of so many things, and I was becoming increasingly certain that I'd never met anyone like her in my entire life—and probably wouldn't ever again. She was a rare gift, and I was thankful that she had come into my life—no matter what happened between us after this point.

Taking my time with her wasn't easy, but I thought it was crucial. I wanted to have a deep relationship with her, not like the casual relationships I was used to having.

"My oldest brother had a dog. Mom would only let us have one pet at a time. James's dog lived until the day he left for college. We all mourned the loss of Petey so much that we agreed never to get another pet again. The sadness was just too much to take." Julia sighed then looked out the window. "I still think about that dog sometimes. He hated thunderstorms and would hide under the closest bed he could find until the storm was over."

"The animals at my home aren't exactly my pets. I've never gotten attached to any of them, since I don't spend any significant amount of time there. I have no idea what it feels like to lose a pet." I thought about that for a moment and thought how shallow that sounded.

Too many things about me felt shallow. I needed to add some depth in my life. I knew Julia was the reason I was thinking that way. I wanted to be everything she'd ever want in a man.

I wanted to be perfect for her, because I thought she was perfect for me.

CHAPTER FIFTEEN

Julia

I t wasn't a real date, and I knew that in my head, but my tummy didn't seem to get the message, and the hundreds of butterflies that flew around in it didn't either. Looking at my reflection in the mirror, I took in the professional hairdo I'd gotten at the salon. Pulled into a fancy up-do, tendrils hung in loose curls around my face. The aesthetician at the salon had done my makeup too. Artimus had sent over a dress and heels, along with a set of diamond earrings and a necklace to match.

Turning to look at Bethey, I asked, "Who am I?"

"One lucky bitch," she joked with me. "Man, this job is really taking you places, Julia."

Spending so much time with my boss was making me feel a deep connection with him. I knew dancing the night away in his arms would only make our connection that much more profound. But I'd yet to tell my roommate anything about how I'd been feeling about Artimus.

Now seemed like the perfect time to let her in on my little secret.

"This job really is taking me places, Bethey. Places I never dreamed it would. Like to a place where I'm falling for my boss."

Her expression turned serious in an instant and she shook her head. "Do not. I repeat, do not act on that, Julia. This is a dream job. Don't let a crush ruin it for you."

"It's more than a crush," I told her as I turned away from her to put my heels on. "I'm almost entirely head over heels for Artimus. Sure, I'd be crushed if he didn't return those feelings, but I also understand how amazing my job is. I don't take any of this lightly."

"Has he told you he has feelings for you, Julia?" she interrupted me.

"No." I slipped on one high heel, teetering on it as I slipped the other one on too. I had to practice walking in them so I wouldn't embarrass myself by walking around like a newborn calf. "Help."

Bethey came to me, taking my hand and placing it on her shoulder. "Steady there, girl." Walking out of my bedroom, we went to the living room, where there was more space for me to get my bearings. "If he hasn't said anything to you about having feelings for you, then don't you think that means that he doesn't have any for you?"

I wasn't entirely sure about that. "I don't know. This is new to me." I wobbled and nearly crashed before regaining control. "Damn, these things are so high. Six-inch heels are new territory for me. I can't believe Artimus sent over these stilts and expects me to dance with him in them."

Bethey looked a little surprised. "Wait. He said he wants to dance with you at this thing?"

"Yes." I looked at her, thinking that her eyes were a little too wide and that she looked a little too worried.

"That's not good, Julia. I thought he only asked you to go with him because he didn't want to have to go looking for a date on such short notice. Now he wants to dance too." She shook her head. "I don't like this. I foresee an ending where you're fired or feel like you have to quit because you two have an office fling, and then when things end, so does your job."

"You can see all that?" I asked her then laughed. "Didn't realize you had psychic abilities, Bethey."

"I don't." She rolled her eyes then let me go. "Take some steps without using me as your support."

Somehow, I managed to walk across the room on my own. "Yes!"

She sat on the sofa, watching me as I kept walking. "Messing with your boss is a terrible idea. I've just got to tell you that, Julia. A coworker is bad, a boss is terrible."

But Artimus was more to me than just the man I worked for. "I genuinely care about him, Bethey. And he seems to care about me too."

"Seems to?" She shook her head again. "Just trust me when I tell you that messing with your boss would be disastrous. Trust me on this."

The alarm on my cell went off in my bedroom, telling me I only had five minutes until Artimus would be picking me up. "I've got to use the bathroom and make sure I'm ready to go. He's almost here." Hurrying as fast as I could, which wasn't fast at all on those heels, I made my way to the bathroom. "If he comes before I'm out, let him in —and be nice, Bethey."

"Oh, I'll be nice. You don't have to worry about that." She snickered, and I wondered what the hell that was about, but didn't have time to ask.

Only a few minutes later, while I was putting on another layer of antiperspirant, I heard her let Artimus in, and then a few seconds later she came into the bathroom. "He's here, huh?" I asked.

She nodded and came close to me to whisper, "Fuck, he's hot!"

"I know, right?" I held her hands as we jumped up and down and giggled quietly.

"I can see why you're falling for him." Then she stopped jumping, and her smile faded to a frown. "But seriously, don't let things get out of hand. You can't mess around with that man, no matter how many muscles he has. And it looks like he's got more than any man I've ever met. And try not to look at him too much, because he's just too great looking. Remind yourself all night that you're so lucky to have this job and that you won't do anything to jeopardize it."

With a sigh, I nodded. "Okay. I've got to go, Bethey. See you later tonight."

"Have fun," she said, then added, "but not too much fun. If you know what I'm saying."

I did, and didn't want to think about what she was saying.

Going out to the living room, my jaw dropped at my first look at Artimus. Artimus at work was already enough to set off all my hormones, but Artimus in a tux was a sight to behold. "Wow."

He came to me, taking my hands in his as he looked me over. "That dress does look amazing on you. Just like I knew it would."

He'd sent over a daring red dress that went to my feet but had a slit on one side that went all the way up my leg to the lower portion of my hip. A tiny thong was the only thing between me and the dress. I couldn't even wear a bra with it, as it had plunging Vs in both the front and the back. As revealing as it was, it still looked sophisticated and glamorous, and I didn't mind the extra skin one bit. It made me feel sexy and fabulous. That's all that mattered to me at that moment.

He let get of my hands and then put one of his on the small of my back. My insides melted at his touch as we headed to the door. He called out over his shoulder, "Bye, bye, Bethey. It was nice to meet you."

She came out of the hallway, waving like a little kid with a smile plastered on her lips. "Bye, Artimus. It was nice to meet you too. You guys have fun. But not too much."

I was thankful when he closed the door behind us. "Why doesn't she want us to have too much fun?"

With a shrug, I acted like I didn't have a clue. "How should I know? Bethey's a little odd sometimes."

On the ride over to the event, it was hard not to gawk at Artimus, so I chose to look out the window more than I looked at him. We made light conversation as we rode the ten miles to the hotel the event was held at.

Artimus took my hand in his, helping me out of the car. His arm slipped around my waist as he leaned in to whisper, "You're much too beautiful for me to let go of tonight. I don't want any men to bother you, so I'll keep a hold on you. If that's okay with you."

It's more than okay.

"Sure, Artimus. Thanks." I didn't want him to think I might get getting any other ideas about why he might be holding that way.

Dinner was served, an auction was held, and then the dancing began. Artimus swept me up with the very first song. "Shall we?"

Thankfully, I'd mastered the heels by that point and could not only walk with ease but dance pretty well too. The way he held me, the way his body swayed with mine, the way he smelled ... it all had me dancing better than I ever had.

Our bodies seemed to have been made to fit together. With the heels on, our hips were on the same level. His hand was on the small of my back, the other held mine against his shoulder, and our bodies touched from the waist down.

The way his blue eyes held mine made me want to kiss him. Of course, I didn't do that, but I wanted to. His lips parted. "Are you having a good time, Julia?"

"I am." I had to smile. "This might be the best night of my life, Artimus. Thank you for asking me to join you here tonight."

A few lights flashed, and I looked around to find they'd let in the paparazzi. Several of them were taking pictures of us. "Smile for them, Julia."

I did as he'd said but wondered how his family would take seeing him in pictures with me. "What will your sisters and friends think about you taking me out like this?"

"That's not something I'm worried about," he answered, seeming unfazed by the question. "And you shouldn't be either."

"Okay." I let that thought go, but then a new one came to me. *What will Price think?*

He'd already accused me of digging into Artimus's pockets. Would he try to ruin this?

And what was *this* anyway?

It felt more like a date than a business event. Especially with the way we danced all night and then laughed all the way back to my place.

"You and I will have to go out dancing more often. We make a great pair." He twirled one of the tendrils of my hair. "Your hair looks so pretty like this."

I palmed one side of it. "If it weren't just a bit too fancy to wear like this at work, then I think I'd wear it like this every day."

He nodded. "That is too bad." The way he gazed at my hair made me think he must be feeling the same way about me as I was about him.

But neither of us seemed to be willing to take the chance and just say what we felt. I knew I wasn't going to be the first person to admit I had feelings for him.

And then there were Bethey's words to consider. *Disastrous* was by far the worst one of those words.

Would it really be so bad if we were together?

I hated that I let myself think that way. Artimus wouldn't settle down with me, so there was no point. I was fooling myself.

The car stopped in front of my building, and the driver opened the door. Artimus got out and reach back in to help me out. "I had a good time, Artimus ..."

His finger touched my lips. "Save it. I'm walking you up. You can tell me what a nice time you had after I get you safely home."

"You don't have ..." His finger stopped me once again.

"Hush. You know I'm not about to send you up to your apartment alone." He took my hand, and that was that.

At my door, he held out his hand for my key. I gave it to him, and he unlocked then opened the door. He moved back and I stepped inside. Giving me the key back, he smiled. "I had the best time tonight, Julia. Thank you."

"Thank you." I froze as he leaned in. I thought he might be about to kiss me.

One hand went to my shoulder and then his lips pressed against my forehead. "Goodnight. Have a good weekend." And then he left me standing there breathless.

If that little kiss could send me into a state of arousal so deep that I felt the wetness pooling in the little bit of material that made up my tiny panties, then what would a real kiss do to me?

CHAPTER SIXTEEN

Artimus

Julia's body in my arms, the way she moved with me, how beautiful she looked—it was all too much to bear. The moment my lips touched her forehead, my cock sprang to life.

All the way back to my apartment, I tried to get that erection to go away by thinking all kinds of un-arousing thoughts. None of them worked. Her effect on me was too much, and I went straight to my shower as soon as I was inside my apartment.

I could still smell her on my clothes as I took them off. Her face filled my mind as I stepped into the shower, the warm water falling all over my hot body.

I leaned back on the tiled wall, taking my cock into my hands. Imagining that I had kissed her sweet lips instead of her forehead, I drifted away to a place where only she and I existed.

Visions of a moonless night on a deserted island greeted me, a waterfall flowing over us as we made love underneath its clear water. "Baby, I've waited forever for this moment," I whispered to her before plunging my cock into her hot cunt.

Her soft moan filled my ears as she wrapped her legs around me. I pushed my hard cock into her as deep as I could get it. Over and over I plunged into her, until she was screaming my name.

Her name came out of my mouth then. "Julia, you are mine. You always have been. You always will be."

Her cunt was squeezing my dick as I moved it inside of her, but I wanted more from her. I wanted to feel every part of her. Pulling out of her, I moved her to get on her knees then slammed my cock into her ass.

Julia made a soft purring sound as I fucked her in the ass. She was even tighter there, making me come before I knew it.

My eyes fluttered open as I spilled my cum onto the shower floor. Panting, I watched the thick white strands go down the drain. "Damn it."

Why couldn't I just be honest with the woman? Why was I doing all this pussyfooting around? This wasn't like me at all. I wasn't acting like myself, and I had no idea why that was.

Wrapping a towel around my waist, I went to my bed and fell onto it.

I should just call her. I should just tell her how I feel.

My head lolled to one side as I looked at my cell sitting on the nightstand. "Just call her."

I didn't move. I knew I wasn't going to call her. I knew she wasn't ready for me.

But how do I know that?

As I lay there, trying to figure out how I could be so certain about so many things about Julia, I found myself really looking at the young woman. There was a naiveté to her that showed just underneath the surface of her professional exterior, and that innocence shone through to me.

In every fantasy I had about Julia, there was an underlying theme. *Forever.*

I'd never thought about being with anyone forever. So why her?

She was much younger than me. Her whole life was ahead of her.

What would she want with a man my age? Would she want forever with me?

I had never been the kind of man who had insecurities. This was new to me.

And then the reality of the situation hit me. I was afraid that if I told her how I really felt, she'd tell me she didn't feel the same way. Those words would shatter me if they came from her mouth.

If I asked her to be mine forever and she came back with any reply other than yes, then I thought I might just fall apart and vanish into thin air. And that made me think that I must be going crazy.

No woman could make me feel like less than the man I was. I'd spent a long time working to become the man I was, and I'd never been less than proud of myself. So how was Julia making me feel like this?

Nothing made sense. And yet, everything seemed so simple.

Dancing with her that night, I'd never felt more like a part of another person. Our bodies moved together in a way that I didn't know was possible. Even though I'd purposely picked out shoes with a six-inch heel that would bring her up close to my height, I'd had no idea how it would feel to have her body that close to mine.

Our hips had been on the same level. The constant contact wasn't only arousing; there was something else too. Something I had never felt in my life. It was as if we were connected even though we weren't doing more than touching.

Not that I felt like my cock was inside of her. It wasn't like that. It was more like we were plugged into each other somehow. She felt so familiar in my arms. Everything about her felt familiar to me.

I'd wanted to kiss her so damn bad when I left her at her door. I'd wanted to scoop her up and take her to her bed and take her dress off, then kiss every last inch of her perfect body.

But I didn't do any of that.

It wasn't the right time. I could feel it somehow. I'd never been that in tune with myself, much less anyone else. And I was at a loss as to how to explain why that was.

The paparazzi had taken enough pictures of us that I knew I'd be getting some calls soon about who the girl was. My sisters would be on me right away, asking me to let them meet her.

Will I let them?

I'd brought less than a handful of women around my family. I didn't like to mix family with the women I dated casually. But I wasn't dating Julia. She worked for me. She'd gone to that event with me as a favor.

Julia, being the consummate professional she always was, wouldn't have put me in a spot to have to find a date last minute. That was the only reason she'd agreed to go with me.

So why had I done that to myself then?

Again, I looked at my cell. "Maybe I should just call her and ask what would've happened if I had asked her to be my date tonight instead of asking her to go with me to help me out."

My eyes closed. I wasn't going to allow myself to call her. The poor girl was probably exhausted from how much I'd made her dance with me. She was sure to be asleep.

I'd already taken up so much of her personal time. Saturdays and Sundays were her days off, and I'd dared to intrude on one of them.

"I'm an ass." I threw my arm over my face.

Selfish. Selfish. Selfish.

I hadn't even thought about Julia needing her time off. Instead, I'd only thought about having her with me, dancing with her, having everyone think she was my date.

"What's wrong with me?" I had to ask myself out loud.

I should've asked her out properly. And I shouldn't have been monopolizing her time either. She was spreading herself so thin for me. It was then that I realized I'd been taking advantage of her.

This was Julia's first job, and it was a much better position than most new graduates obtained. She'd do anything and everything she could to make sure she'd get to keep that job. Including going out with me.

I'd become the thing that I had most loathed. I was being the boss who asked his employee, a woman he was attracted to, to do more than what would normally be asked of anyone else in her position.

Going out on a date, even if I had worded it differently, was going too far.

No, I hadn't threatened her with anything to get her to accompany me. No, I hadn't pushed her at all to join me. But she was young, eager to keep her job, and eager to please her boss.

And I had taken advantage of that.

This was exactly the kind of situation I had wanted to avoid by putting in place such harsh rules at the station. How I ironic was it that I was the first one to break the rules so atrociously?

I knew I had to make things right, but I didn't have the slightest clue how to do that. Maybe just backing off would be the best thing. I certainly couldn't keep up my plan of showing her that I wanted more from her, not now that I had realized what I'd been doing.

As I lay there, silently berating myself, a thought occurred to me. I had to adjust my behavior immediately and make sure I was never asking Julia to do more than her job required.

No more late nights that ended up with her spending the night at my place. No more spur-of-the-moment invites, like needing a date for something. None of that.

Can I still take her to lunch?

I nodded. Yes, that would be acceptable, and would even be an appropriate way to show how much I appreciated all the hard work she'd done for the station and me.

But overall, I had to back off. I had to give the girl some breathing room. I hadn't done much of that, having kept her with me as long as I could each day.

It was selfish, but I was happy to have figured that out before it had gone too far. But even with that realization, I knew I still wanted more from her. I felt like a pretzel inside. Wanting her with one part of me, but wanting to make sure she didn't feel pressured with another part of me. Wanting to treat her the best way I possibly could as a boss. Wanting to treat her the best way I could as a man who found her stimulating, arousing, and completely capable of stealing my heart and making it her own.

What a mess I'm in.

Rolling over, I got underneath my blanket and tried to settle in to get some sleep. I had a hell of a lot of thinking to do before Monday came and I saw Julia again.

Maybe I could try to think about as if she were one of my younger sisters. It was worth a shot, wasn't it?

Just as I had determined this new course of action, her face appeared in my mind. Long dark silky hair hung around her gorgeous face. Pouty lips begged to be kissed.

No, I can't think of her the same way I do my sisters. That's out.

Was the task of putting my feelings for Julia behind me impossible? Was it impossible to think of that woman as only my employee? Should I do something about that?

But what could I do about that besides fire her?

I couldn't fire her. Not only because I liked her so much, but also because she was damn good at her job. It also wouldn't be fair to her, or even legal.

The time had come for me to do whatever I had to for this to work. I could do it. I'd done hard things many times in my life. I could make sure I treated Julia like any other employee, only expecting her to do her normal job. That meant not exploiting my position to get her in my home, and especially not my bed.

But I'd keep up with the nice things I'd been doing for her. Having meals brought into the office that she'd actually eat, and letting her keep the shopping account so she could get new clothes. Those were things I'd keep giving her.

It wouldn't beat myself up over continuing to have feelings for her, mostly because I knew they weren't going to go away. But I would stop trying to make our relationship more personal, even the things I'd been doing on a subconscious level.

I'd seen the light. That meant things had to change.

CHAPTER SEVENTEEN

Julia

The rest of my weekend was so busy that it felt like a vacation when I finally got back to work. And I was surprised to find that Artimus had beaten me to the office. He stood in the lobby, talking to Brady about something when I stepped off the elevator.

A bright smile that reached all the way to his eyes greeted me. "Hey, Julia. How'd the rest of your weekend go?"

After giving Brady a nod and a wave to say hello, I headed toward my office, and Artimus joined me. "Sunday was full of house cleaning, laundry, and generally busting ass."

I opened the door to my office, and he came inside with me. "Sorry about that. I should've thought about everything you needed to do this weekend. I'm sure the outing on Saturday evening put you behind on whatever you'd had to do at home. At the very least, I should've sent over one of the maids to do all that for you."

Taking the seat behind my desk, I noticed that Artimus was frowning. "Yes, going out on Saturday did put me behind." I stopped to think about all the fun I'd had. "But I would gladly get behind again if I got to do a repeat of Saturday. I had the best time ever, Artimus. Thank you again for asking me to go with you. I'm glad you waited until it was too last-minute to invite an actual date."

His expression changed to one of surprise. "You are?"

Is he kidding? "Of course. That was a once-in-a-lifetime kind of thing for me. I seriously doubt I would've ever gotten to go to anything like that if you hadn't taken me to it. My mother thought it was so nice of you to take me too. I told her all about it."

"And she wasn't angry that I had you go with me on one of your days off?" he asked with worried eyes.

He wasn't acting like himself. "Artimus, why would she be angry about that? It was a once in a lifetime opportunity. Who cares what day it fell on? Not me, that's for sure. And I had the best time ever. Mom couldn't believe I danced all night long. I have a reputation in my family for being a bit of a klutz."

"I couldn't tell that at all. You were light on your feet." He took a seat on the other side of my desk, looking much more relaxed than he had been a moment ago. "And I had the best time ever too. But I won't be bothering you with things like that anymore. I was wrong to put you in a position where you had to sacrifice your personal time for me, especially when it hardly had anything to do with your job. I realized that later that night. I've been asking too much of you, Julia. I'm sorry for that."

What the hell is he talking about?

"Artimus, I really mean it. I had the best time with you Saturday night. I felt like a princess. Why would you say that you're sorry for making that happen for me? I don't understand." My hands fisted in my lap, feeling that there must be something or someone behind this sudden change of attitude. Maybe even someone who didn't want us to be together at all.

I thought Saturday night had really shown how great he and I were together. We had a connection that couldn't be denied, yet there we both were, denying it.

He leaned up, putting his elbows on my desk then holding his chin on top of his fists. "Can I ask you to be perfectly honest with me, Julia?"

"I am always honest with you, Artimus." I waited for his question and wondered what the hell had happened for him to be thinking this way all of a sudden.

His blue eyes peered into mine, and he wore the most serious expression I'd ever seen on his handsome face. "Did you agree to go with me to that event just to please me?"

Had I?

He'd asked me to be honest, so I gave him an honest response. "Artimus, I do like to please you. That said, I wouldn't go just any place you asked me to. I thought the charity event sounded amazing. And it didn't disappoint me at all." I decided to be even a bit more honest than that. "I liked that you felt that you could ask me to do that. And I'd love it if you asked me as often as you'd like. I really did have the best time. And the sweet kiss you gave me when you left me at my door was nice too." I tried to say that in the most professional manner I could, while also trying not to blush.

The worry vanished from his face, replaced by happiness. "That's good to hear. I spent the rest of the weekend worrying that I'd been asking more out of you than is acceptable for the job. Promise me that you'll let me know if you feel like I'm overstepping any boundaries. I don't mean to. To be honest with you, I truly enjoy your company, and that's why I've been taking up too much of your time. But I'll stop doing that."

Stop?

"No, don't stop doing what you've been doing." I reached out to take one of his hands. "I enjoy your company too. I haven't felt put out even once. Let's not change a thing. Please, boss." I squeezed his hand as I smiled at him. "And please don't feel guilty or worried about a single thing."

He blinked, long and slowly, before asking, "Do you really mean that? Or do you just think that's what you need to do and say to keep this job?"

I had to laugh. I hadn't done a thing wrong with the job I'd been given. "I've never once felt that my job is on the line. I don't need to do a damn thing I don't want to in order for me to keep this job. I haven't made one mistake since I started here. There are no grounds to fire me, and I'm not jumping through any hoops to keep it." I hated that he thought I was only spending time with him because I wanted to make sure I kept my job.

His entire demeanor changed. Artimus sat up, tall and confident. "Good. Then let's get to work, shall we?"

Glad to have things back to normal, I opened up the laptop that was sitting on my desk. "I'll get to checking out the weekend ratings."

He got up, heading to the door that joined our offices. "And I'll get on checking out the quarterly reports. We're both going to be busy until lunch, so I'll order in something around noon. Okay?"

"Sounds good to me." I watched him leave my office, closing the door behind him. Then I shook my head, still not understanding what had prompted him to bring up our earlier conversation.

Did he really think I was just kissing his ass to keep my job?

The thought was ludicrous.

Only fifteen minutes had passed when my office phone rang. Looking at it, I hated that I had no idea who would be on the other end of that line. I picked it up. "Julia Bengal."

"Hey." His voice sent chills through me.

My hand gripped the phone, wanting to crush it. "What do you want, Price?"

His tone turned stern, "I want to know why you and your boss were out on the town this weekend. I thought you said nothing was going on between you two. Did you lie to me, Julia?"

My temper flared. "Let me get this out of the way. Price, you are nothing to me. I have no reason to lie to you. And what I do with anyone is none of your business."

He cut in, his voice deep and threatening, "Listen to me, Julia. I always get what I want, and I want you. I'll fight Moneybags if I have to. He won't win, I can promise you that. I've got the perfect job for doing the man in. Is that what you want? For Artimus Wolfe to end up a victim of the tabloids with hundreds of women claiming he's sexually harassed them?"

Now I was beyond pissed. "That would be a lie, Price. Would you really stoop so low as to make shit up about a person just to get what you want? And just so you know, no matter what happens, I'll never be with you again. So don't waste your time and reputation to try to bring anyone down. It won't get you what you're after anyway." I paused in my rant, wanting to make sure he knew something else. "If anything is put in print about Artimus Wolfe, I will go straight to the authorities and let them know about this threat, Price. Don't fuck with me. I'm a nice person as long as I'm dealing with nice people. If I'm not dealing with a nice person, I can be their worst nightmare. My advice to you is not to push me to hurt you."

He huffed. "You don't scare me, Julia."

Shaking my head, I couldn't believe what a jackass he was. "You should be scared. I mean it. I won't be your victim anymore. You need to get it through your head that what we had wasn't much and now it's over. You have yourself to blame for that. And don't call me on my cell or this office line again." I slammed the phone down before putting my head in my hands in frustration.

I heard the door between our offices open and then Artimus asked, "Is everything okay, Julia? I heard you shouting at someone."

Lifting my head, I looked at him. His expression was one of concern. "Everything is fine, Artimus. Thank you for asking."

Coming to me, he placed his hand on my shoulder. "Julia, you can tell me anything. If you need help with something, or if someone is bothering you, or even if you just want to talk, I'm here for you. I am more than just your boss; I'm your friend too."

My hand moved before I realized what it was doing. It traveled all the way up to rest on his hand, which still lay on my shoulder. "I know you are. It's just some old friend who used to be in my life but isn't anymore, and he's not too happy about that. I shut him out, and every once in a while he tries to get back in."

He gave my shoulder a little squeeze. "What did he do to get you to shut him out?"

I wasn't about to admit to him or anyone else that Price had hit me. I shook my head. "I'd rather not talk about it. It's nothing, really. I just didn't like the guy anymore and didn't want to spend any more time with him, and he can't seem to take no for an answer."

With a huff, he said, "Maybe you should tell me who this man is, so I can make sure he knows you're done with him and he needs to move on. And if he can't move on by himself, then he can move on with my foot up his ass." He moved his hand to rub my shoulder. "If you tell me who he is, he will leave you alone. I'll make sure of that."

I was pretty sure Artimus could follow through with that promise. But I didn't want to tell him the real reason I didn't want Price Stone in my life any longer. If I asked him for his help, one day I would have to tell him what had happened.

"Thank you, Artimus. I tell you what, if the guy gets any worse, I'll definitely ask for your help. Right now, he's just bugging me." It wasn't the truth, and I knew that. Price was escalating, making open threats. And not just about me anymore, but about Artimus. I should've told Artimus all about it.

Why does admitting that someone hit me make me feel so damned ashamed of myself?

CHAPTER EIGHTEEN

Artimus

A few days had passed and I hadn't heard Julia shouting at anyone over the phone again. The man who had bothered her seemed to have gotten the message finally.

I had to admit that hearing about the guy made me feel even more protective of her and even somewhat jealous, too. I knew she didn't want anything to do with the guy, but at one time she must've.

Going into her office, I found it empty and wondered where she'd gone to. I headed down the hallway to Lila's office. Julia had gone down there quite often to grab a cup of coffee and chat.

I could smell the coffee before I got to the door, and I took a moment to take a deep sniff, loving the way it smelled. Julia always brought me back a cup, but I was in need of some caffeine now, so I thought no one would mind if I went in and grabbed my own cup that morning.

Lifting my hand to knock, I stopped as I heard one of the ladies inside shout, "You're a what?"

Julia's distinct laugh traveled through the door. "Nina, don't look at me like that."

Lila asked, "Do you have strong religious beliefs or something? Is that why you're still one?"

One what?

"Not religious beliefs," Julia answered, "but spiritual ones. That's why I'm still a virgin."

She's a virgin?

My cock sprang to life, growing at a rapid pace. I turned to hurry back to my office, knowing I wasn't in any state to walk into that room.

I knew I shouldn't have been listening in on a private conversation, but now that I knew Julia was a virgin, I couldn't unlearn that bit of information.

By the time I got back into my office, my cock was throbbing, and I went to my private restroom to take care of the situation, knowing that nothing else could make it go away. Leaning on the wall, I released my erect member and went to work on it.

Julia's face sprang up in my head, her role in my fantasies so familiar that it happened without effort now. Her lips moved, telling me she was a virgin and that she wanted me to have her special gift. All I could do was groan at the idea while beating my meat to oblivion.

I had to have her now. Leaving her alone wasn't an option anymore. I had to make Julia mine. And I didn't want to wait any longer.

In my fantasy, Julia began to strip away her clothing as I sat at my desk, watching her. She trailed her long fingers over her body, dipping them between her plump breasts, then all the way down to her innocent pussy. "You want this, Artimus?"

"Yes," I growled. "I want that virgin pussy."

A smile took over her face. "Good. Because I want you to have this. I want you to be the first man to show me what sex is like."

"The only man," I said before getting up and bending her over my desk. Running my hand over the pristine flesh of her ass—an ass that had never been touched by anyone before—I felt a surge of energy moving through me.

It felt as if a river of pure sexual energy had risen up from the depths of my groin to flow through her, connecting us in a way I'd never imagined. Taking her by the hips, I held her still as I pushed my cock into her virgin hole. The tightness was incredible.

"Yes," she hissed. "Finally."

Finally, she'd no longer be a virgin. Finally, only my cock would penetrate her soaked cunt. Finally, we'd both gotten what we wanted.

Fucking her without seeing her face wasn't enough for me. I had to watch her as I made her feel things she'd never felt before. I pulled out then turned her over. Picking her up, I laid her back on the desk then pulled her to me, thrusting into her once more. This time I could see her face light up every time I stabbed my cock into her tight pussy.

Her eyes held mine as I moved in and out of her while playing with her exposed clit. "You know exactly how to touch me, Artimus."

"You know how to take me so well, baby." I thrust my hips, going in deeper.

"Ah!" she moaned as her eyes closed.

"That's right, baby. Close your eyes. Get lost in this moment." I moved at a furious pace until I felt her tight pussy clench even tighter as she came to a climax.

Her eyes flew open as she grabbed each side of the desk, experiencing her first orgasm. "God! Artimus!" Her body shivered and shook as she came unglued.

The way her tight cunt clenched around my cock did me in, and I came inside of her tender pussy. The first time she felt a man's hot sperm coating her insides, and it was mine.

Huffing and puffing, I ejaculated into the toilet instead of her. I leaned my forehead against the cool tiled wall and tried to catch my breath.

How long could I hold out, now that I knew she had held out for so long? Knowing that she'd been hanging onto that bit of innocence that most people seemed to be in such a hurry to get rid of only made me crazier about her. I had already been in deep before, but this news brought out something primal and inexplicable in me.

My hands were shaking as I washed myself off in the sink. No one had ever made me shake with anticipation before.

And why was I letting myself think that I would definitely be the one to get her virginity? I had no idea why I was setting myself up the way I was.

What would happen if she didn't choose to give it to me?

I'd be deeply disappointed, to say the least. At the very worst, I would be devastated. I had to calm down. I had to get back to reality.

The woman had kept her virginity intact for some reason. If I I'd overheard correctly, she'd said something about the reason behind it being spiritual.

What the hell does that even mean?

Was she saving herself for God?

Who did that? Besides, she had told me before that she wasn't religious.

I splashed my face with cold water to try to bring myself back to the here and now, instead of the fantasy world I'd just been in.

In the real world, people didn't hold onto their virginity for no reason. In the real world, there were deeply held beliefs and convictions for someone to wait as Julia had.

There was no way she was going to just let me have what I wanted, which at this very moment was her spread-eagled on my bed, letting me take that gift from her.

I was fucked and knew that without a shadow of a doubt.

Would getting Julia into bed mean having to marry her first?

Looking at my reflection in the mirror, I shook my head. "You cannot ask a woman to marry you just to get into her pants, Artimus Wolfe."

You can if you love her.

Staring into my own eyes in the mirror, I didn't recognize the man who was looking back at me. "Who are you?"

Thoughts were coursing through my mind that were completely unfamiliar to me. Julia and me walking down an aisle that was covered in red rose petals, heading toward a man at the end of it. He'd say some things, then ask us to repeat them, and at the end of it all, we'd be man and wife. And then he'd tell me to kiss my bride.

I would kiss her then pick her up and carry her away with me. All the way to the nearest bed, where I'd strip the white wedding gown off her beautiful body that was now mine in God's eyes.

She'd welcome me with open arms, and I would lay my naked body on top of hers before penetrating her slowly, making her all mine and only mine.

I slapped myself to tear myself away from this idiotic illusion. "What the hell is wrong with you? That girl won't marry you right now. Hell, you haven't even let her know you'd like to date her."

So, do that then.

Could I do that? Could I go to Julia and just spit it all out?

How hard could it be?

I could just talk to the girl. I could simply tell her that I was interested in getting to know her on a romantic level, and that I'd like to start dating her ASAP.

But how long would a virgin want to date before she'd agree to get married and give her innocence away?

Years!

I nodded as I looked at myself in the mirror. "Years, Artimus. Can you wait for years?"

The only thing that kept echoing in my mind was the word *no*.

No, I couldn't wait years to taste her sweetness. No, I couldn't even wait months for that to happen.

So, what the hell was I going to do about that?

Is it possible to speed up the dating process?

Putting everything back into place, I zipped up my pants, ran my hands through my hair, and then went out to sit at my desk. Business was the last thing on my mind. I was all into planning out the shortest possible courtship so that I could get to the good part.

Thinking about how Julia and I had been spending our time together, I gathered that we had pretty much been dating for a month or so already. We ate most of our meals together. She had stayed the night at my place. We'd gone out to a charity event together, dancing the night away. There were even pictures of us holding each other as we danced that had been put into newspapers, tabloids, and social media, too.

As far as anyone on the outside could see, Julia and I were already a couple.

Could I point that out to her, thus giving us a month of dating as credit for how we had spent our time together?

Was that something a spiritual person would do? Accept credit on relationships?

I had no idea what being spiritual really meant. Did it mean she was into ghosts? Did it mean she thought of herself as something other than merely human?

I had no idea, and I had even less of an idea of how to ask those kinds of questions without sounding like an idiot.

My cell rang, and I saw it was Duke. Swiping the screen, I answered the call with a question, "How do you get a virgin?"

"What?" came his astonished reply.

"A virgin, Duke. How do you snag one of them?" I asked as I shoved my hand through my hair, feeling like I was teetering on the edge of insanity.

"Should I ask you why you've got that on your mind?"

"No. You should just tell me how you get a woman, who has held on to her virginity for spiritual reasons, to give herself to you." I waited for his answer. I was sure Duke Cofield, ex-professional football star, would know the answer to that. The man had been a ladies' man back in his heyday, after all.

"Um, how do I say this, Artimus?" He paused a bit before adding, "I've never been with a virgin. So I can't help you there."

Well, crap!

Not even he knew how to get a virgin to give it up.

I was in over my head. I knew that now.

There would be no getting Julia to see things my way. I would just be wasting my time. Not only that, but I would be risking the incredible relationship we did have if I told her how desperately I wanted to sleep with her.

On one side there was a huge rock, and on the other side was a hard place. I was stuck between the two.

Without a soul to guide me, I wasn't going to go anywhere with Julia.

CHAPTER NINETEEN

Julia

L eaving Lila's office with a cup of coffee for Artimus, I went to my office and straight through to his, only to find that he wasn't there. It was getting close to noon, so I figured he'd gone to lunch with someone.

He'd been ordering out and having lunch brought to the office for a while now. So it did seem a little odd that he'd go out to eat without saying a word to me about it.

Taking the coffee with me, I went back to my office and sat down, getting back to work. I would skip lunch, since I didn't really like to eat at any of the nearby cafés. They didn't have the kind of food I liked to eat anyway.

I looked at my computer screen, not taking in any of the information that was staring back at me. My mind was on Artimus, wondering where he was and what he was doing.

Only then did I realize how much I enjoyed our lunches together. Without ever asking me about what I wanted to eat, he would always order dishes that I didn't even know I'd like, but would inevitably end up loving.

He and I would talk about anything other than work while we ate. It was a nice time that I looked forward to each day.

But maybe he didn't want to do that anymore. Maybe that time was over for us. I didn't like to even think about that.

A knock came at my door. "Hey, it's Lila. Come eat with us, Julia."

I pressed the button to open the door and found Lila and Nina standing there, waiting for me. Nina waved at me to come with them. "Come on. We're not taking no for an answer this time."

Sitting in the office feeling sorry for myself wasn't what I should be doing anyway. So I got up, grabbed my purse, and went with them. "Thanks. My usual plans for lunch don't seem to be happening today anyway."

Nina nudged me with her shoulder. "You mean your little lunch dates with Artimus?"

"I wouldn't call them dates, Nina." I bumped her back with my shoulder.

Lila laughed. "Why not? Everyone else does."

I was shocked. "They do not!"

Nina laughed too. "Come on, Julia. You and he stay holed up in your offices more than you are out of them. And what about those pictures that have been floating around of you two at the Humane Society charity event last weekend? You looked quite at home in his arms."

"Did I?" I feigned surprise. I knew I'd looked that way. I'd seen the pictures too, after all. Who could deny the fact that I looked and felt at home in Artimus's arms?

Lila and Nina laughed at me as we got onto the elevator. Lila punched the L button to take us all the way down to the ground floor. "Has he made any advances, Julia?" Lila's smile was crooked, as if she already knew the answer.

But there wasn't anything to know. "No, he hasn't. Artimus is always the perfect gentleman." Sometimes I wished he wasn't though.

Sometimes I wished he would just throw me over his shoulder and take me to his bed, where he'd make short work of my virginity and tell me—much like a caveman would—that I belonged to him and no one else.

Sure, it sounded like something a woman from the dark ages would say, but at times I really did wish for him to do something like that. Taking the decision out of my hands would be the best thing Artimus could do for me. He wouldn't hear any arguments from me, because that's exactly what I wanted too.

We walked over to an Italian eatery, where the carbs would be forced down my throat. But I didn't say a word about the restaurant choice. Instead, my focus went to the table of men who sat near the back of the establishment.

Lila smiled as she looked at me. "Oh, would you look who's here. What a complete surprise."

Nina and I leveled our eyes on her. Lila had known damn well those three men would be there. They just so happened to be seated at a table for six. That couldn't just be a coincidence.

As we walked straight to them, Duke got up and pulled out a chair for Lila, the two of them sharing a quick kiss. "There you are, baby," Duke greeted her.

Nina and I took chairs next to each other as Ashton moved to take the seat by Artimus. "Here you go, ladies." He smiled at Nina as he sat by her. Only Artimus and I were separated, and I was put out with myself at how quickly I'd noticed such a thing.

"Hi there, boss," I said as I sat down.

"Hey," Artimus said as he looked at the menu in his hands.

The waiter came to give us menus then took our drink order. I looked it over, finding very little that I would eat. I still hadn't found anything to my liking by the time he came back to take our orders.

One by one, the others rattled off what they'd be having, and then it came down to me. "Um, I think I'll just have the salad."

Artimus cleared his throat. "Or you could try the salmon in dill sauce. She can get that without the bed of rice, right?"

The waiter nodded. "Of course." He looked at me. "I can have the rice substituted with some steamed broccoli, if you'd like?"

"That would be great. Thank you." I put my menu away.

After the waiter left us, Lila pointed out, "Seems Artimus knows your diet better than you do, Julia."

Artimus wasn't about to let that statement go without saying something about it, "Julia knows she wants to keep her carbs low. She just doesn't know a lot about what foods are the best for that." He looked at me with a frown on his face. "And unfortunately, she thinks she's got a battle with her weight to win. I keep trying to tell her that she's already won and that she should find a better diet to help her maintain her goals."

Having heard Artimus give me a similar speech multiple times in past few week, I decided to do something I'd never done before. I picked up my purse and took out a picture of my family and me from a few years back. Handing it to Nina, I said, "Here you go. Pass that around so everyone can see why I'm such a freak about what I eat."

She looked at the picture and her eyes went wide. "Oh."

My mother, father, older brothers, and I were all obese. Not just chubby. Obese. The rest of my family didn't seem to care about that and had never bothered to change the way they ate.

When I moved out and went to college—my first experience away from home and my mother's fatty cooking—I took the initiative to start living a more healthy life. I knew I wasn't always perfect at it—not eating enough was just as bad as eating too much, as Artimus had helped me realize—but I tried to make the best of it.

"Artimus is right. I don't know a lot about the foods I can eat. All I knew for sure when I started making my own meals was that salads were something I could eat as much as I wanted. And in the beginning, while my stomach was still shrinking, I ate four bags of premixed salad each day." I patted my flat tummy. "It took a whole year to get to a healthy weight. It took another year of exercising every day to get the loose skin to go away. So, yeah, I take what I put into my mouth very seriously."

When the picture got to Artimus, he stared at it then looked up at me. "You sure did work hard to get to where you are today, Julia. I find it impressive and inspiring."

I was a bit embarrassed, but I wanted everyone to know that I didn't have an eating disorder. I had genetics that gave me a reason to watch what I ate, and I was tired of everyone thinking other things about me.

After lunch, I was ready to get right back to work. "Artimus, we should get going," I reminded him. "We've got that FCC meeting in an hour."

With a nod, he got up. "I'll take care of the check and see all of you tomorrow."

I walked out in front of him as he called his driver to meet us in front of the restaurant. Artimus hadn't been nearly as talkative as he usually was. I wondered if that had to do with seeing my old picture.

When we got into the back of his car, he still wasn't back to his normal self. In fact, he was acting even odder. He stared out the window instead of talking to me. It felt awkward. So, I finally broke the silence. "Did seeing the picture of me bother you?"

He looked at me then shook his head. "No. Not at all." A smile curved his lips. "If you want to know the truth, I found you beautiful in that picture."

So that's it. He's into bigger women. No wonder he hasn't made any moves on me.

But I wasn't about to gain weight just to please him. The fact was that I felt better in every way being at a healthy weight. No one was going to get me to change that about myself.

"Well, what has you acting so strange then?" I asked.

A long sigh came out of him as he looked at me. "I accidentally heard you talking with Lila and Nina today. I'm sorry, but I can't unhear what was said."

I knew what he'd overheard in an instant, and heat flushed my skin from my head to my toes. I knew I'd gone crimson. "You know I'm a virgin?"

He nodded, and I covered my face with my hands. I was so embarrassed.

Artimus pulled them back to make me look at him. "Don't be embarrassed about that, Julia. It's not an easy thing nowadays. But could I ask you a question about it?"

Why fight it? It was out there. What else could he ask me that would be any less humiliating? "Go ahead." I rolled my eyes. "The cat's out of the bag now, after all."

Without an ounce of shame, he gave me a sweltering once-over. "Why are you still a virgin? I mean, you're smoking hot, and I know men have been after you."

And here's where I'll lose my chance of ever having this man.

"Because I'm waiting for the right one—the man I'll be with for the rest of my life. I don't want to have sex with men, I want to have sex with one man. For the rest of my life. I know that sounds archaic, but that's just the way I feel."

I expected to see surprise in his eyes, but he didn't change his expression at all. "Do you think you'll ever find that man, Julia?"

I already had, but just didn't know how to say it. I nodded. "I do. I really do." *It's you, Artimus.* But the words wouldn't come out of my mouth.

His eyes weren't leaving mine. His chest heaved as he took a deep breath. "Do you think you might've already found him?"

It's you! It's you!

My brain could say all kinds of things that would never leave my lips. I had no idea why that was. All I knew was I couldn't make myself tell him the way I really felt.

If I could've, I would've told him that I thought he hung the moon and stars. I thought he was the best-looking man I'd ever seen. But not just that, he was the best man I'd ever known. Inside and out, he was gorgeous. I'd be lucky to have him. And if he saw fit to give himself to me, then I would gladly give myself to him.

But men didn't like to think about giving themselves to women. They liked to think it was the woman who gave herself to them. In my version of a happy relationship, both parties had to give themselves freely and equally to the other. Nothing could be one-sided. Both had to give it all up, letting the other know they were in it with complete abandonment. Letting go of everything to make sure the other knew they were their entire world.

It was a lot to expect, according to most every other female I'd ever told that to. But it was what had been in my head forever, so to me, it was entirely achievable.

I gave him my answer and hoped he would read into it. "I have. But he doesn't know that yet."

CHAPTER TWENTY

Artimus

S itting there, looking at Julia, I had a strong feeling that I was the man she was talking about. But what I didn't know was if I was truly ready for everything that went along with being with her.

My fantasies and dreams had already been full of thoughts about being with her and only her. But she hadn't yet told me a thing that would truly let me know that I was the man she was referring to. I could've been wrong. She could've had another man in mind.

I knew she wasn't dating anyone. Or I thought she wasn't, anyway. "Are you seeing anyone, Julia?"

"No." She bit her lower lip, and I thought she might be about to confess all about this mystery man who had so captivated her. But then her cell phone rang.

She looked at it then hit the button, sending it to voicemail. I noticed an angry look on her face. It wasn't a look I was familiar with seeing on her pretty face much at all. "Who's that?"

Not meeting my gaze, she shoved the phone back into her purse. "No one."

If I knew anything about Julia, it was that she took her time letting people know things about herself. Like the weight thing. It had taken her over a month to tell any one of us about her struggle with obesity. I had a feeling that she was struggling with another situation that she'd take a long time to tell anyone about.

Taking her hand, I wanted to make a physical connection with her to let her know I wasn't just some random stranger. I was Artimus, her friend. A person she could trust—if she'd only allow herself to do so. "How come you don't want to let me in on who keeps bugging you?"

Her eyes were glued to our clasped hands. I felt her palm begin to sweat. When she gulped, I knew there had to be something wrong. Or something very right. I wasn't sure which it was at that moment. "It's not something I want to bother you with."

How could she think I would be bothered by anything about her? Was I not being as open with her as I thought I was? I mean, I knew I wasn't telling her how I felt about her, but other than that, I was an open book. Or at least I thought I had been like that. "It's bothering me more that you won't tell me anything about this guy. It's the same guy who called you at the office, isn't it?" I knew it was. Or at least hoped it would be. I didn't want to think about Julia having more men in her past who were overstaying their welcome in her life.

Did she have a habit of seeing someone then suddenly deciding they weren't the man for her? She was clearly looking for a very specific connection, so did she dump men without any warning when she realized they weren't the one? Did her commitment to her ideals about love and a relationship make her to cut men out as soon as the smallest problem arose?

Those were all intimidating thoughts. Mostly because I knew problems would arise in any relationship, and if she was the type to think that one little argument meant we weren't right for each other, then I had a real problem on my hands.

After making me wait for her answer for what I deemed to be a bit too long, she finally said, "Yes."

Thank God!

There was only one man in her past. Or had it been? I had to ask, "So, is this guy the only man you've ever dated?"

With a nod, she answered me, "Yeah. I've been asked out a lot. And I have gone out on what I would call group dates. You know, where lots of people are going to the same place or function. I can't put my finger on why I accepted this man's invitations to go out, but I did. And when I didn't want to anymore, he got mad."

"Mad?" I was a little confused. I knew I'd get mad too if she cut me off without so much as a reason why. And I couldn't truthfully say whether or not I'd be able to stop myself from hounding her for answers. "Did he threaten you or something like that?"

"Um, no." She seemed to be hesitating, weighing what she would and wouldn't tell me. "He just wants me to give him another chance."

"And you don't want to do that?" I had to ask. "Why don't you want to give him another shot?"

She shrugged. "Because I see no use in doing that." She looked at me, her eyes shining with that now-familiar inner wisdom. "We had our thing. It wasn't anything spectacular. There were no sparks, no fireworks. But that's not exactly why I ended things, though. He's aware of why, and it's a pretty damn good reason. I don't see the need to open up that book again, expecting a different ending this time. Do you understand what I'm saying?"

"You think that what happened to make you dump him in the first place would probably happen again." I knew what she was saying, even if I didn't know the exact reason why she'd had to end things with him.

Nodding, she said, "I know it would. I knew it when I dumped him, and I'm even more certain from the way he's been treating me in the time since we broke up. He can't change. And even if he could, it still wouldn't matter to me. I know he's not the guy for me. I've told him that again and again. If you want to know the truth, I think he's just obsessed with me because I'm a virgin. I think it's driving him nuts that he didn't get that from me." She huffed, her arms crossed over her chest, closing herself off. "That was never going to happen, and I told him that right from the start. I let him know that I liked his company, but I could tell that he wasn't the man for me, so nothing physical would ever have happened between us."

I was happy to hear that. "So, you two never did anything at all? Not even kiss?"

Secretly, I hoped she hadn't even kissed another man. But I knew that was a longshot.

"We did kiss." She looked down and moved her hands to her lap, clasping them together nervously. "He got me to make out with him a few times. He said it wasn't fair of me to just say no to having sex with him if I wouldn't allow him to show me what he could do for me physically. So I let him show me a little, and when it didn't affect me the way he thought it would, he was more than a little disappointed."

I was glad she didn't feel anything for the guy, but also a little worried about her lack of a libido. I mean, who could make out with someone and not get aroused?

"Was this guy unattractive?" I asked her.

She laughed. "He was very attractive. He was charming, even. I honestly couldn't say a negative word about the man when we first met, and that's part of why I started dating him. He had a great career, made a great living for himself. He had nice things. One could almost say that he had it all. He just wasn't for me. I wish he could've under-stood that before he went too far. I wish he could've understood that the reason I wasn't going to have sex with him was about me and not him. The last few months, I've realized that he wasn't as great as he first seemed, though, and that he feels like he missed out on a piece of virgin ass that he could gloat about to his friends."

I began to wonder where this guy was. "So, is he here in New York?"

"Yes."

That made think that this guy was too close not to worry about. "Is he harassing you?" I asked.

She pursed her lips, thinking a little too hard for my taste. It was a simple yes or no answer I was looking for, but that was not what she gave me. "Somewhat," came her confusing reply.

Somewhat?

It wasn't an outright yes, but it was more than I wanted to hear. I didn't want anyone messing with her or harassing her in any way at all. "I can take care of that for you."

Her dark hair flew around her shoulders as she shook her head. "No. Stay out of it. Please. I don't want to make any trouble for you."

Now, what would be the trouble in making sure this jackass knows I won't allow him to fuck around with this woman?

I took her by the hand again, stroking my thumb over the top of it. "Julia, it's troubling to me that you're being harassed by someone."

Lifting her eyes from our hands to look into my eyes, she whispered, "Why?" There was so much behind those eyes. Even more than I was used to seeing from her.

And with that look in her beautiful eyes, I came clean. "I care about you. A lot."

She still didn't understand what I was saying. Or at least wasn't allowing herself to dig deeper into my words. "Why?"

I took her by the chin, running my thumb along her jawline as I gazed into her eyes. "You're perfect, that's why."

We stared at each other for quite some time before she asked, "Do you really think so?"

I was going for it. Putting everything out on the table. I didn't want anything left unsaid. "I do. I've thought that since the moment I met you."

"I think you're perfect too, Artimus." The words were even sweeter than I'd imagined. "I don't want you to worry about that stupid ex of mine. He's a pain in the ass, but I can take care of myself where he's concerned."

I couldn't care less about that ex of hers now that I knew she thought about me the same way I thought about her. "You think I'm perfect too?"

She nodded. "But you're my boss. And no relationship is set in stone. I don't want things to go south and have to quit working with you. I really love my job."

I thought it best to go along with her for the time being. I now knew what I'd been desperate to know before. She was into me.

Giving it some more time would only make it hard for her to ignore the fact that we were meant to be together.

"Yeah, it's best just to keep things the way they are between us for now, I guess. But I want to know if that guy goes too far. No matter what, I don't want you to get hurt. Promise me that you'll tell me if things start to get out of hand, Julia."

"K." She bit her lower lip, her chest heaving as she breathed deeply. "Artimus, can you make me a promise too?"

I could promise her the moon. "Anything."

"No matter how much it feels like the right thing to do, don't kiss me." Her eyes were glued to my mouth as she said it. "I don't think I could come back from that."

I was glad to hear that, so I told her whatever she wanted to hear. "I won't. Mainly because I don't think I could come back from that either. So, does this mean I've lost my dance partner?"

"No, you haven't lost that," she answered, shaking her head. "You haven't lost anything we've already done. And at least we've admitted there's an attraction. But we know it can't go anywhere."

"Okay. Glad we got that out of the way." I knew everything I needed to know then. The attraction was mutual, and both of us knew that one kiss would ignite a fire that would never burn out.

CHAPTER TWENTY-ONE

Julia

Seeing Bethey as I walked into our apartment, I found myself feeling rather chatty. "Hey, you'll never guess what happened to me today, Bethey."

Picking up the glass of red wine she was already halfway through, she cocked one eyebrow at me. "Let me try to guess, Julia. Um, you got to meet some big celebrity?"

I shook my head. "Even better than that." I went to the kitchen to grab myself a wine glass and filled it to the brim with the wine she'd left open on the counter.

"Better than meeting a celeb, huh?" She ran her finger around the rim of her own glass. "Okay, did you find a hundred dollar bill on the sidewalk?"

Laughing, I went to sit down with her on the sofa. "Nope. You'll never guess. Let me just tell you about it."

"Okay then." She nodded at me. "Shoot."

I felt giddy, my insides all wiggly as I let her in on my news. "Artimus is into me."

She rolled her eyes. "You think that's news, Julia?"

"Well, yeah, I do." Pulling the glass to my mouth, I took a sip while my roommate laughed her ass off.

"How can you be so smart and so dumb at the same time?" she cackled away, nearly falling off the sofa.

"I don't see why you think I'm dumb, Bethey." I got up, picking up her now empty glass and taking it to the kitchen. "No more wine for you. You've had plenty."

She stopped laughing to look over at me as I washed out her glass. "Oh, come on. You've got to know that he and you have had the hots for each other since day one."

Going back to take my seat again, I said, "That may be true, but today we told each other how we feel."

She went silent, her eyes wide. "Julia, this isn't good at all."

I knew her warnings about dating the boss. "Don't worry. We're adults, Bethey. We agreed that it wouldn't be smart to date while working together. And I don't want to quit my job. So, we won't be doing anything about the attraction. Even though I really think he might be the one." I sloshed the wine in my glass, looking at the legs it left on the glass. "I'm not stupid. I know my ideas about relationships are a bit intimidating for most people, Artimus included."

"And he's aware of all of this?" she asked me with some concern.

"I've told him what I want in a man," I said with a nod. "And he knows I'll only ever share my body with one man." I took a drink of the wine to steady myself. "And he didn't jump in and say he'd be what I needed. He's not ready to make the kind of commitment I want."

Bethey tapped her fingers on the table next to her. "Did he tell you straight up that he wasn't interested in seeing you exclusively?"

"No. But we didn't let it get that far. I said that no relationship is set in stone and that I worked for him and wanted to continue doing that, so we'd have to put the attraction to the side. And he agreed." I put the wine glass down to think about that for a minute.

Bethey was already on it though. "He agreed?" She shook her head. "I don't see a man like that agreeing so easily to not moving forward if there's really an attraction there. And I know there is. He's got a plan, Julia. Artimus Wolfe, the great and powerful billionaire turned network mogul, has something up his sleeve, and you're going to have to be very careful now that you've admitted everything to him."

Could she be right? Had I misread him? Would Artimus set some type of a trap for me now?

And if he did, would I really give a crap if I fell into it?

My go-to fantasy of him turning caveman on me rose up in the back of my head. "I'm going to take a long hot bath then hit the sheets, Bethey. If you need to use the bathroom, now's the time."

"Okay," she said as she got up. "That wine has filled my bladder up entirely."

I headed to my bedroom to grab my robe and a towel. All the while, I had to wonder if Artimus really did have something up his sleeve like Bethey had suggested.

Finding a bath bomb I'd gotten at Christmas, I took it with me as I headed to the bathroom, which Bethey had by now vacated. I filled the tub with hot water then threw in the bomb. An aromatic blend of lavender and a bunch of other flowers filled the room.

After stripping off my clothes, I climbed into the tub, settling in for a long, relaxing soak. Dunking a washcloth into the water, I wrung it out then placed it over my face, covering my eyes.

With my body so relaxed, it was easy to let my mind slip into an alternate reality. One where only Artimus and I existed.

He was there with me, in the bathtub. His hard body was behind mine as his large hands moved over my arms, his lips grazing the side of my neck as he whispered sweet nothings to me.

I'd never had sweet nothings whispered to me. I had no idea what words they actually were. But I would've bet anything that Artimus would know how to ignite a fire inside of me using nothing more than his little words.

With my body between his legs, I could feel the lump of his swelling manhood against my lower back. Heat pooled between my legs, and my body yearned to feel that hot piece of flesh between his legs, inside my most intimate areas.

Turning to face him, I moved my legs to straddle his body. His hard cock pressed against my apex. "Artimus, I am yours."

His hand ran up my back, taking hold of my neck and pulling me to him. His mouth was hot and demanding as he kissed me. Our tongues did battle before his overtook mine, claiming it, making it his.

His hands moved to my waist, lifting me up then sliding me back down on his erection. My body shuddered with desire as he entered me. My breath caught in my chest as he impaled me with his long, massive organ.

As if the gates of heaven had been opened, I could feel the rush of energy flow through me as he filled me so completely. He moved me up and down, stroking his cock with my body. Slowly, almost agonizingly slowly, he moved my body.

His mouth released mine and I pulled back to look at him. His bright blue eyes penetrated mine. Though we used no words, his gaze told me exactly what he was thinking. It told me that I was the only one for him and that he was the only one for me. No one would ever come between us. We would always be as one.

My lips trembled to feel his on them again, and he pulled me back into his arms to give me the kiss I yearned for. The way the water moved around our bodies served to enhance the electricity that flowed between us. Each lap of water against my flesh seared it.

I moved on my own to stroke his cock now as his hands moved away from my waist, up my back, until he had two handfuls of my hair, pulling it back, forcing our lips to part. He kissed a trail down my throat, over my collarbone, then took one tit into his hot mouth.

A hiss escaped me as he bit my nipple. My cunt clenched around his cock at the pain, though it hurt in a way that pleased me to no end. "Devour me, Artimus."

Biting and sucking my tit, he made my arousal grow with every nip. I arched my back as an orgasm ripped through me. Although my body pulsed around his cock, he didn't let go yet, continuing his assault on my breast.

As soon as his mouth left that area, I nearly wept with the loss. I moaned with pleasure as he bit the other nipple. "Yes!"

Artimus growled as he gnawed my flesh. The man had an animal wildness inside him, hidden beneath his human exterior. As he feasted on me, my nails raked across his back as another orgasm hit me like a tidal wave. I shrieked with the sensation, which nearly took me under it was so intense. "Yes! Artimus, yes!"

My body shook as I came back down. All the while the animal in Artimus only grew. He pulled his mouth off me before moving me off him. I had no idea what he was doing as he got out of the bathtub and reached in and picked me up as if I didn't weigh a thing. "I want to watch, baby."

I still didn't understand but trusted him completely as he took me to the vanity. The long mirror above it cast our reflections back to us. He pushed me to lie on my chest and then thrust his cock into me from behind, holding me down, watching himself in the mirror as he fucked me.

My eyes were glued to his muscular reflection. His body rippled with each hard thrust he gave me. My cunt dripped with desire as he moved his hard cock deep inside of me.

The masterful man who took me from behind made me feel like a goddess. And he was my god.

His dark hair hung in damp strands, sticking to his handsome face. His breaths came out in short huffs with each thrust he made. I'd never seen him look manlier. He appealed to me on every level.

My sweet Artimus could become a sexual master, capable of turning me into his whore who sought only to please her master. He alone would have the pleasure of using my body, in whatever ways he needed to. And his body would be used by mine, allowing me to feel things I'd never felt before. We had more than just a sexual connection; it went to our very cores. And that connection couldn't be denied.

His cock went stiff inside of me and heat filled me. Cum dripped down between my legs as he gave me his seed. I looked at his reflection, his jaw tense, his eyes on mine through the mirror as he claimed me. "Only my seed will ever fill you. Only your cunt will ever receive my gift, Julia. I am yours and yours alone."

"I am yours and yours alone, Artimus." My eyes closed as my body burst with another orgasm.

The sound of my harsh breathing brought me back to reality. I was in the bathtub, my hand between my legs, my finger on my clit. Somehow, I'd just given myself the most intense orgasm of my life.

"My God," I whispered to myself.

I knew that being with Artimus would be beyond imagination, especially knowing that we were invested in only each other. Giving myself to him while knowing that he was the only man for me would be better than any fantasy my imagination could conjure up.

Why do things have to be so damn complicated?

CHAPTER TWENTY-TWO

Artimus

Sitting at the poker table in the bar of my penthouse, the beer had gone to my head. So I started talking about something I hadn't planned on bringing up. "Something kind of cool happened earlier today."

Duke put two cards down, then Ashton gave him two to replace them. "And what would that be?" he asked.

I looked at the cards I held, the queen and king standing out amongst the lower cards. "Julia and I admitted something to each other."

Duke looked at me with a big grin as he tossed in another fifty dollar chip. "Don't tell me. You've both confessed your undying love for one another." The kissy-face he made had Ashton and I chuckling.

Shaking my head, I let him know we hadn't gone that far. "No. But we did admit that there's an attraction between us."

Ashton chunked in a matching chip, and I folded, not having anything good in my hand and not paying much attention to the game anyway. There was only room in my head for Julia.

"Does that mean you two are the newest couple at WOLF?"

"Nope." I sat back and took a long drink of my cold beer. "Julia has a requirement that comes along with dating her. One she's pretty sure I can't abide."

Duke called, and then put his straight flush down on the table. "Read 'em and weep, Ashton. All clubs from five to nine."

Ashton didn't blink an eye as he put his cards on the table. "Hmm, seems I've got one of those too. Only mine are all hearts, and I have the royal family here, along with a ten and an ace."

"Fuck." Duke frowned as Ashton hauled in the three hundred dollar pot.

The smile on Ashton's face wouldn't be going anywhere anytime soon. "So, what's this requirement of Julia's?"

I wasn't sure if I should let them in on something so personal about Julia. Her virginity was her business. But she had told Nina and Lila about it, and either one of them might say something about it. And I did need my friends' advice.

So, I went for it. "Julia is a virgin, and comes with some stipulations."

Both of them raised their eyebrows as their jaws dropped. Then Duke offered some sage advice. "Whatever those stipulations are, do them."

Ashton nodded in agreement. "Yeah, man. Do whatever it is she wants."

I knew they had no idea what Julia wanted. It was kind of fun to inform them. I wanted to see what kinds of reactions I would get. "She wants to have sex with one man in her entire life. She won't be giving her virginity to any man who won't commit to her."

Duke huffed. "Like marriage?"

"She didn't say that exactly." I scratched my head, not even certain myself if she meant we would have to be married or not. "She said she's waiting for the one man who's right for her. She doesn't want to have sex with more than one person, so she's been waiting to find Mr. Right."

"So, she wants you to be with her forever?" Ashton asked with a funny look on his face. "And you guys haven't even dated?"

"Well, she didn't come to me and tell me she wanted me or anything like that. I overheard the girls talking, and that's how I found out about her being a virgin. Later on, when we were alone, I asked her about it. And when I asked her how it was that she was still a virgin, she told me everything. I asked her if she thought she'd found the right man yet, and she said she had."

Duke put his empty beer bottle on the table. "And that man is you, huh?"

"Yep." I leaned my head back on my laced fingers. "But she didn't even bother to ask me if I thought I was the man for her—or if I was ready to make such a huge commitment to her, for that matter. Instead, she said she knew relationships were never a sure thing and that we should just keep things the way they are."

Ashton got up to get us another round of beers. "Can you do that?"

"No." I knew I couldn't do that. "I'm not sure how I'll get her to come around and see reason though."

"And what would reason be, Artimus?" Duke asked as he put the cards in the shuffler.

"You know. What's reasonable." I took the beer Ashton held out for me. "Like not expecting someone to tell you things they don't mean or can't possibly promise. Like telling someone you'll be with them forever. No one can know if they're really going to be together forever."

The way Duke cocked his head told me he didn't entirely agree. "Lila is the only woman I want. She's the only woman I can see myself with. Don't you think that when you've found the right woman, the one you want to see every day for the rest of your life, that you can make such a commitment?"

Do I want to see Julia every day for the rest of my life?

Yes. The truth was that I did want to see her. But I had no idea how long that would last. It was just too soon to even think about something like that.

I looked at Duke as I opened my beer bottle. "You say that, Duke, but if you really feel that way, then why haven't you asked Lila to marry you yet?"

"It's not the right time. But I'm sure I'll know when it is." He pulled the cards out of the shuffler to deal them out to us. "For now we're just enjoying getting to know one another on another level. The level where you get to know a person intimately—and I don't mean sexually either. I mean like in a mundane, human way—their bathroom habits, their personal hygiene habits. Being with them when they're in a bad mood because monthly cramps have made them miserable, and miserable people tend to make those around them that way too."

"See, that's what Julia doesn't understand with her idealistic beliefs." I picked up the cards that Duke had dealt out and was pleasantly surprised with my hand. Keeping my face clear of any expression, I went on, "How can I tell the girl that I'm in it forever when I have no idea if I'll be able to accept her at her worst?"

Ashton shrugged. "You can't. It would be a lie if you told her that now. I can see where you're coming from, Artimus. And I don't envy you one bit. But that's what dating is for. Who says you have to go from nothing to everything?"

"If I can't promise her everything, then why would she risk her job to be with me? Not that I would ever fire her if she broke up with me. But it's a lot more complicated than that." I took another sip of my beer, not feeling satisfied with any conclusion we'd come to.

Duke tapped the table to get us to ante up. "Now that it's been proven that Artimus has one hard road ahead of him with Julia, let us delve into your predicament, Ashton. When are you going to admit your feelings for Nina?"

I jumped in, "Yeah, when are you going to stop denying your feelings and go for it, Ashton?"

Shaking his head, he placed one card on the table, face down. "She doesn't deserve to have to deal with me."

Duke dealt him another card. "And what makes you so bad?"

"Well, there is the tiny fact that at least once a week, I wake up screaming." Ashton looked back and forth between us. "I can't shake what happened. I can't let go of the memory of that accident. I can't let go of the fact that my fiancée died because I was behind the wheel of that car. It haunts me. I feel like being alone forever is punishment for what happened to her. And I feel like I deserve that punishment."

And I thought I had it hard. "You should get help, buddy. You need to see a shrink."

Duke agreed, "You do. What happened is a tragedy, but you can't let it stop you from living your life, man. Nina's a great girl. Why not let her in on what happened and see if she can't be your angel? Having someone in your life might help you remember that it's worth it to get through this and move on with your life."

All Ashton could do was shake his head. "Nina is a great girl. She's happy, fun-loving, and all around fantastic. Gorgeous, too. How could I saddle her with a nut-job like me?"

"Nut-job?" I had to ask. "You are not one of those. You're a man who's had something bad happen to him. You have a scar from it. A mental one."

Ashton shook his head. "Scar? No, a scar forms where the wound has healed. That's what no one seems to understand. My wound is still open. It hurts me all the time. Every day I think about what happened. And sometimes in my dreams, it happens all over again, and it's like the wound is new and fresh all over again. The memory won't go away. It hasn't faded at all. I'm stuck with it and stuck with the guilt, and I don't know if I deserve for it to go away."

"It was an accident. You weren't drinking or on your phone or distracted in any way. You've told us that," Duke reminded him. "It was a slippery road that sent your car skidding across the median. There were trees in your way that caused the impact. It wasn't you. Not in any way was it you who made that happen, Ashton."

Ashton's eyes drooped as he looked down at the cards in his hand. "I wasn't speeding, but I could've driven slower." He looked at Duke. "I had both hands on the wheel, but I could've been paying more attention to the conditions of the road. There are so many things I could've done differently."

I wasn't sure if I should say anything to him or not. But then my mouth opened anyways. "Ashton, do you believe in God?" I asked

His head dropped, and his words came out so quietly I could barely hear him. "I used to."

Duke and I exchanged looks of concern and sadness. He reached out across the table and patted Ashton on the shoulder. "Man, we're gonna get you some help with this, buddy. I promise you that. We wouldn't be any kind of friends if we didn't make sure you got some help with this. It's a soul-crushing thing that you've been through. When something is that tough, no one can do it alone."

My heart hurt when Ashton pulled his head back up. Unshed tears glistened in his eyes. He looked back and forth between Duke and me, his lower lip trembling. "I'm ready. I'll take your help. I'm so ready to get this shit behind me and move on. Help me be the man that Nina deserves. And I can't do it alone; you're right about that."

Clapping him on the back, I assured him, "You've got it, buddy. I'll get on the phone first thing in the morning, and we'll get help for you. You can always talk to us. We'll always be here for you."

As glad as I was that Ashton had finally given in and was going to let us help him, I knew I still had my own dilemma to deal with.

Julia needed to bend a bit, or we'd never get a chance to see what we could or couldn't become. No one could be sure of what life would throw at you. If Julia held firm to her belief, then she might miss her opportunity at love all together.

I had no idea if love was in our future. I knew I loved to be around her. I knew I loved the way her voice sounded. I loved the way she smelled. I loved the way she looked. I loved her attitude and personality.

I knew I loved all of those things, but I didn't know if I loved her. And if I did love her, somewhere deep inside of myself, would that love be enough to last forever?

CHAPTER TWENTY-THREE

Julia

Walking into the office on Monday morning after our little heart-to-heart, I knew it would be awkward to see him.

Two dozen red roses sat on Brady's desk when I got off the elevator. He wore a surgical mask and gloves, complete with protective eyewear. Glaring at me, he pointed at the crystal vase filled with the fragrant bouquet. "These are for you. Kindly remove them and take them to your office before they penetrate my sinus cavities, thus making my allergies go crazy."

Gathering the gorgeous flowers, I just knew they had to be from Artimus. "Good Monday morning to you, Brady. Sorry about your allergies. I'll get them away from you." I took them to my office and placed them on the table near the window. Taking a nice long whiff of them, I pulled the little white envelope off the plastic holder.

My name was written on the envelope in what looked like male handwriting. Pulling the small card out of it, I nearly dropped it when I saw what was written on it.

Julia, I'm not giving up. Don't expect me to. Love, Price

Artimus hadn't made it in yet, thankfully. If he had, then he'd have certainly snooped and read the card. Then he would know that Price Stone was the man who was bothering me. I didn't want him to make the connection between me and Price.

If Artimus confronted Price, then Price might tell him the reason I broke up with him. Not only did I want to keep that to myself, but I knew Artimus would not be pleased, and I didn't know what he would do to Price.

I had to get rid of the flowers, and fast. Hauling ass to Lila's office, I knocked on the door with one hand while holding the vase in the other. "Lila, it's Julia."

The door opened and I hurried in. "For me?" Lila asked with a smile.

"Sure, you can have them. I don't want Artimus to see them." I placed them on her desk. The envelope and card were in my hand. "You've got a shredder in here, don't you?"

She pointed to the closet. "There's one in there." I went to get rid of the paper as she asked, "So, want to tell me what the hell is going on?"

"My ex-boyfriend sent flowers and this note. I don't want Artimus to know a thing about it. Can you keep my secret, Lila?" I pushed the button on the shredder and less than a second later, the note was history.

"Sure, I can keep your secret." She looked at the flowers. "Duke is going to ask questions though. I'm afraid we need to get rid of these too, even though they're really gorgeous."

Jerking my head toward the shredder, I asked, "Think this will break if we use it to shred them up?"

"If we cut the stems off, I don't think it will hurt it." She got a pair of scissors out of her drawer then we set to work, deflowering and de-stemming and then shredding the petals to bits.

The scent of the roses filled her office. "Smells damn good in here now, doesn't it?" I asked.

Lila tossed the last of the stems into the trash before turning her attention to me. She walked toward one of the sofas, taking a seat as she wiggled her finger at me. "Come, sit and tell me why you didn't want Artimus to see those flowers."

After closing the door to the closet with the shredder, I went and took a seat across from her. "On Friday afternoon, while we were on our way to the FCC meeting, he and I talked."

Her eyes narrowed. "About?"

I laughed. "About how he had overheard you, Nina, and I talking when we were having our coffee."

Her eyes went wide. "He knows about your virginity?"

I nodded. "Yep. And he asked me why I'm still a virgin. I told him what I told you guys. And he asked me if I'd found the man I'd been waiting for yet, and I told him I had. He asked if it was him and I told him yes."

"So, you two are a couple now, and you didn't want him to see those flowers and stir up trouble?" Lila asked.

"Nope." I played with the hem of my skirt as I explained our conversation from the other day.

She looked as if she couldn't believe me. "Did you two kiss?"

"No." I knew one kiss would send me over the edge. I would never come back from that. "He's not ready, Lila. I could tell that much. If we had shared even one kiss, it would've evolved into so much more, and I'm too worried about messing up our professional relationship to jump into more so quickly. At least, not without more assurances about the future. I'm not myself with him. I've never had to exercise so much self-control."

Lila pulled her blonde ponytail over her shoulder then ran her fingers through it. "So, he's the one, huh? How do you plan on making things work out then?"

"Ha," I laughed. "Lila, I have no plans and no ideas at all. I don't know the first thing about getting a man to promise me forever. I just know I have to have that before I give myself away."

"Your virginity isn't your soul, Julia." Lila sighed as she pushed her hair back again. "In my opinion, if you want to get Artimus where you can keep him, you're going to need to give in at least a little. Date, make out, make him want you so badly he'll promise you the moon. How else will either of you know for sure that you're right for each other if you don't explore your relationship a little before making bold declarations?"

She was right. I could go about it like that. "I don't want to just entice him into doing what I want. I want him to want it too. If he doesn't, then maybe he isn't the man for me."

A frown filled her pretty face. "Julia, that's not how people work. Your expectations are too high. I'm afraid you're going to end up all alone if you keep striving for this ideal man. Artimus is a great catch, and he may well be the man for you. You two have a real connection. Anyone can see that. I say give the man a chance to prove he can be what you need him to be. But you're going to have to give some of yourself to him first. And I don't just mean your body, though a little bit of physical intimacy wouldn't be the worst."

"I don't know how much of that I can do. For as long as I can remember, I've believed a man would come along for me, and we would just instinctively know we were made for each other. It's hard to think about it in any other way."

Everything I was saying to Lila was true, but there was a little more to it as well. I was almost certain that Artimus was the one for me—crazy ideals and all. No one else had ever come close to making me feel the way I did for him. But what if I was wrong about it all? About Artimus. About my ideas of love. That would be devastating to me.

With a huff, she said, "That's a fairytale, Julia. There is no man who can live up to those standards you've made up in your head. It's not even fair to ask anyone even to attempt to do that. It sounds like you're talking about fate, and you can't hold one person accountable for that."

"Well, I do expect that." I had no idea how to tell her how important it was for me to hold onto these standards.

"Perhaps Artimus can make you change your mind about that." Lila got up and made a call, asking Nina to join us.

Moments later, Nina strolled into the office and got a pot of coffee brewing. Lila was quick to deliver my news, and then I had two females telling me that Artimus would never offer me forever without me doing much more first.

For the first time in my life, I was wavering. I didn't want to be alone forever, but I was starting to see how that might become a possibility, as they were saying. But I didn't want to compromise myself either.

"What if you two dated for a while, Julia?" Nina asked.

"I'm not saying we couldn't. But I think that he would get sexually frustrated, and that would lead to a breakup. That would make working with him difficult, and I would most likely hate it so much that I would quit my job." I nibbled on my lower lip, growing increasingly apprehensive about everything.

Nina agreed, "Men do get sexually frustrated pretty easily. I can see that happening." Her eyes met mine. "What about oral sex? Will you do that with him? That might alleviate the frustration and solve that problem."

"Sex is sex in my book. There would be no oral sex. The most I'll do is kiss. No playing with my boobs, no touching his dick. Nothing that would make it seem like I might change my mind and have sex." I shook my head, thinking about the last few nights I'd spent dating Price.

I knew that I thought differently about most people when it came to these things, but I didn't understand why people never believed that I meant what I said. So many people—Price was just the latest—just assumed that they could change my mind about everything. There might be a few things that I would be more open to, but in my experience, anytime I looked to be giving an inch, someone was ready to take a mile.

Just as I was considering whether I could take that kind of risk again, there came a knock at the door. "Hey, it's Artimus. Is Julia in there by any chance? I can smell the coffee and was pretty sure she'd be here."

The girls looked at me, and Lila whispered, "He's here for you, Julia."

Nina poured two cups of coffee and handed them to me. "Here you go. You and Artimus have a nice morning now."

I took the coffee to the door then opened it. "Hi there, boss."

The way he looked at me melted my heart. "Good morning, Julia."

I offered him one of the cups. "Coffee?"

He took it with a smile. "You know it."

We walked, side by side, down the hallway. "How was your weekend?"

He smiled as he blew the steam off the top of the cup. "It was okay. And yours?"

"Nothing special." I stopped at my office door.

"Come to mine." He moved in behind me, placing his hand on the small of my back to guide me one door down. "I'd like to talk to you about something."

Just that little touch was making me a hot mess, especially after spending so much time just moments earlier thinking about the real possibility of letting my relationship with him progress. We weren't even in his office yet, and I had envisioned me laid out on his desk as he took me from behind, holding me down by the shoulders, trapping me.

I had no idea why I kept thinking he would ever be so domineering with me—so demanding with my body that it was almost animal. Artemis wasn't that kind of man. He would wait for my approval. He wouldn't push me at all.

We stepped inside, letting the door close behind us. He steered me toward his desk and put his cup of coffee down before taking mine away from me and putting it down too.

His hands crept up my arms. One stayed on my shoulder, the other cupped my face. "I can't stop thinking about you."

Then tell me what I need to hear, Artimus.

I didn't say that. I needed him to come to terms with that on his own.

"I've thought about you a lot too." I moved his hand away from my face, as it was making it hard for me to think. "And so far, I still think we should keep things the way they are. I don't want this to end with us not liking each other."

He grinned at me with a sexy expression. "I don't see that happening."

But I did, and I wanted him to see that too. "Here's how I see it if we're not perfectly honest and careful about this, Artimus. You and I date. We kiss, to the extent that I will allow myself to, which isn't much by normal standards. You end up getting frustrated, and we end up not liking each other. The end."

"Or what if we kiss and then those barriers you have just melt away?" He took my hand, pulling it up to his lips.

I felt the burn deep within me as his lips touched the top of my hand. I knew my resolve would disappear if our lips met. My words were breathless when they came out. "They would. And I can't have that."

24

CHAPTER TWENTY-FOUR

Artimus

J ulia managed to stay busy and stay away from me for most of the day. She even went so far as to go to lunch with Nina, instead of eating with me.

I knew she was afraid. I couldn't tell her I was ready for forever yet, but I could offer her one hell of a great time until I knew for sure one way or the other what I could give her.

The end of the day was near. I didn't want her to leave and just let the whole day go by without us saying anything else to each other. I thought about who I knew in town and came up with an idea. One phone call got me an invitation sent my way, and Julia would soon get the email about it.

Only minutes later, she rushed into my office. "Artimus, I have no idea why this invitation came so late, but you've been invited to the mayor's mansion for dinner this evening."

Feigning surprise, I asked, "What time, and is there a plus one on the invitation?"

She looked at the paper she'd printed out. "Yes, there's a plus one, and it's in two hours."

"Well, order a dress and have it sent over. Call my maid and have her give my driver a tux to bring to me."

"I've already got one coming your way as we speak," she said, ever the efficient assistant. "I called her before I came to tell you about this."

"Good. So get a dress, get to hair and makeup downstairs, and we'll go to this dinner." I got up, taking her by the shoulders and escorting her back to her office before setting her down in her chair. "Get the dress ordered right away, Julia. And make sure it's an expensive one. I want you to look amazing tonight."

She huffed then waved me away. "Go on then. Leave me to it, Artimus."

Smiling all the way out the door, I was feeling very proud of myself. We would be spending the whole evening together. *Mission accomplished.*

An hour and a half later, I met Julia in the lobby on the ground floor. When she stepped off the elevator, wearing a little black dress and heels to match, my breath caught in my throat.

Her dark hair was in a sexy pile on top of her head. Her makeup was perfect—red lips and cheeks, golden eyeshadow that made her gorgeous eyes pop. She waved at me as she came my way. "I'm ready."

I stood right where I was, unable to move. "My God, you're beautiful, Julia."

"Thank you." She looked me over. "You always make a tux look nice, Artimus."

I was so mesmerized by her beauty that I couldn't move until she walked past me. Then I shook myself out of it and followed her like Pepé Le Pew. Julia had no idea how gorgeous she looked.

The dress wasn't daring at all, with its boatneck collar that went all the way up to the hollow of her throat. A long rope of pearls spilled down the front, all the way to about where her bellybutton would be. The bottom of the dress hit her just above the knees, and the sleeveless style showed off her well-toned arms, too. The sexiest thing about the dress was how it fit her form precisely, clinging to the curves of her breasts and accentuating her small waist, before blossoming over her round hips and bodacious ass. The black six-inch heels made her legs look long and lean, the way a thoroughbred's look. I couldn't take my eyes off her.

My driver held the car door open for us, and she got in first. I slid in right beside her, close enough for our legs to touch. I reached across her to put her seatbelt on and she smiled at me as I did. "I can do that, you know."

"Um, hmm." I clicked it shut. Moving back past her, I slowed down when our faces were very close. "You smell like jasmine."

"It's a perfume the makeup girl had. She spritzed me with it—said it went with my look." She took a sniff of the crook of her arm. "I like it. I'll have to ask her what the name of it is so that I can get some."

I already had plans to ask the makeup girl myself and beat Julia to it. I would give it to her as a gift, along with some flowers, and maybe a box of dark chocolates too.

Would jewelry be too much?

I wanted to give the girl the world.

Her hand lay in her lap looking lonely, so I took it into mine, cradling it on top of my thigh. "I missed seeing you today. You made yourself quite busy. Was that so you didn't have to be around me?"

Looking down, she blinked a few times before answering. "Maybe." She looked at me with longing in her pretty brown eyes. "This isn't as easy as I thought it would be."

"No, it's not." I grazed my knuckles across her cheek. "Maybe we should stop pretending."

She shook her head. "I don't think we're pretending at all. We're being very honest with each other."

I didn't think either of us was being completely honest. "Are we?"

She couldn't look me in the eye for some reason. Her head was slightly tilted, and she looked out the window instead of at me. "Yes."

"Then I'll ask you again. Do you know the man you want to give yourself too? The man you want to spend the rest of your life with?" It was selfish and I knew it, but I wanted to hear her say it again.

Now her eyes came back to mine. "I do."

She wasn't telling me exactly what I wanted to hear, so I pushed further. "Is he in this car right now?"

She looked down, letting out a long sigh as she did. "Let's not do this, Artimus. It serves no purpose. You know you're not ready for anything long-term. And I'm talking very, very long-term. I'm not ready to give up on my dream of being with only one man, but I know I can't trust my body to follow my head around you."

Just hearing her say that, I knew she was right. I wasn't ready to tell her I wanted her and only her forever. Not yet. So I didn't push it any further, but there was something else I wanted from her that I think we were both ready for. "Let's just have a nice night then. It's not every day that one gets to dine at Gracie Mansion with the mayor of New York."

Finally, a smile pulled at her lips. "I know. I'm so excited."

Running my arm along the back of the seat, I wrapped my hand around her shoulder then pulled her close to me. "So am I. And just so you know, tonight you are my date. Not just my companion, my actual date." I kissed her cheek and felt my lips tingling right away. "I have to admit something to you, Julia. I've known the mayor for years, even before he was elected. He went to high school with my father. The two were good friends. I made a call and got us an invitation to dinner tonight because I wanted to spend the evening with you."

She placed her hand on my chest, looking up at me. "Artimus, you're such a sneak." The smile never left her face. "As sweet as it is for you to call me your date, I don't think it's a good idea. Like I said earlier, I'm afraid you'll start to expect certain things from me if we start dating. I don't want to disappoint you in any way."

It was about the kissing thing. She was afraid if we kissed that she would lose her resolve. "If I promise not to kiss you, then can I call this a date?"

"Dates typically end with at least one kiss, Artimus." She shook her head. "No, you can't call this a date. We are not dating, and that's that."

Her stubbornness on this told me she truly was afraid that she might give herself up to me before she was ready. Even without me making the commitment to her that she needed. That was a good sign in my books. Eventually, she wouldn't be able to deny what was between us any longer.

The car slowed to a stop and I looked away from her to find we'd arrived at the mansion. "Here we are then, platonic friend who came with me as a favor." I had to laugh. No matter what she wanted to call it, we were out together. In my opinion, that was a date—whether I kissed her or not.

We got out of the car and she shivered. "I didn't realize it was this chilly." She put her arms around herself to warm up.

"I can't have you meeting everyone with goosebumps." I wrapped my arm around her, pulling her close to my side as we walked up to the door, where a butler waited for all the guests to arrive.

Once inside, the cold air wasn't bothering her anymore, so she tried to pull away from me. "It's nice and warm in here. You can let me go, Artimus."

I didn't want to though. "I don't mind."

With a laugh, she took the hand I had around her shoulders and peeled it off her. "I do. You have no idea how you affect me, do you?"

I had every idea how I affected her because she did the same thing to me. I let her have her way though, removing my arm from her and feeling the loss right away.

A staff member approached us with a bright smile on her face. "Hi, I'm Tammy. The mayor told me to ask you two if you would like a tour of Gracie Mansion before dinner is served."

Julia clapped her hands. "Yes. That would be great, Tammy. I'm Julia, by the way, and this is …"

Tammy put up a hand, stopping her. "I know who both of you are. Artimus Wolfe, owner of WOLF network. And you are his assistant, Julia Bengal. I saw pictures of you two not too long ago, from when you attended the Humane Society Ball. You make an attractive couple."

"We're not a couple," Julia was much too quick to point out. "We work together so closely that it's just easier to go to events like the ball and this dinner together. It saves Artimus from having to find a date at the last minute."

I placed my hand on the small of her back, leaning in to say quietly, "I don't think you need to explain things so completely, Julia. Just say thank you when someone gives you a compliment." I looked at Tammy. "What she means to say is thank you, Tammy. Please proceed with the tour. I've never been here before either. This should be fun."

With a smile and a nod, the girl led the way as I steered Julia to follow her. She looked up at me with a fire in her eyes. "Would you mind terribly removing your hand from my back?"

"Why?" I asked with a sexy grin. "Is my touch making you desperate for more?"

"Rogue," she hissed.

Maybe I was a rogue. Maybe I wasn't playing by her rules, but she had too many rules in my opinion. Maybe it was time she met a man who refused to play by them.

Maybe I was that man.

CHAPTER TWENTY-FIVE

Julia

D inner was awesome. And that was something I didn't say often. Not until meeting Artimus Wolfe, that was. If nothing else, the man had been able to introduce me to some pretty great foods.

To start the meal we had a small salad full of fresh veggies, some thinly sliced strawberries, and toasted pecans, drizzled with raspberry-balsamic vinaigrette. They served white wine with that. When the filet mignon was served next, we were given a glass of red wine to accompany it. And when the tiny lemon custard was served, we were given a stout coffee with sugar and cream. It got rid of the little buzz the wine had given me.

Bidding everyone a good night, Artimus and I got into the backseat of his car. His smile was bright as he looked at me. "It's too early to go home. And we look too good to end this night now. How about we hit a club, Julia? I'd love to do some more dancing with you."

I wasn't about to go out on a work night, and I shook my head no. "We've got to get up early for work tomorrow. I'm not up for a night out then work tomorrow. Sorry, Artimus."

Slipping his arms around me, he leaned in. The masculine scent of him cologne made my heart speed up. "You're with the boss. I think I can arrange a sick day for you and me both. So, what do you say? Wanna go out dancing with me?"

"A sick day?" I asked. My body was already heating up as I thought about spending a night in his arms, swaying to the music or dancing to a hard beat.

He nodded, making his dark waves move around his face. "A paid sick day."

No loss of income. No loss of sleep. No reason to say no.

"Okay." I had to smile as I watched his grin grow even bigger.

"Okay." He pushed a button to lower the glass between the driver and us. "We'll be going to Output tonight."

"Yes, sir," the driver said, then Artimus rolled the tinted window back up.

Artimus looked at me with a wry grin on his handsome face. One hand moved up my arm, the other went to my hair. "How about we let your hair down, Julia?" With a few swift moves, he let my up-do down, my hair falling around my shoulders. "Yes, that's better. The other way was nice for dinner. This way is better for dancing, free and a bit wild."

Wild was how I imagined Artimus in all of my fantasies about him. And it seemed he wanted to show me a bit of the animal I was sure lay just beneath his manicured surface.

When we pulled up to the club, I saw people standing in a long line that went all the way around the corner. "We'll never get in."

He laughed as he pulled me out of the car with him after his driver opened the door. We skipped the line, going straight to the front. The doorman gave us the once-over then let us in without asking a thing.

I assumed Artimus was easily recognizable and known as a man of great wealth, a man who would spend lots of money in the place. That was the only thing that made sense to me.

The vibrations filled my body before we even got into the main area where a DJ was playing music for a crowd of undulating bodies.

Artimus had taken my hand when we got out of the car, and he didn't show any signs of letting it go. He pulled me along with him to the nearest bar. Holding up two fingers as the bartender looked our way, he said, "Two zombies."

Moments later two tall glasses filled with some yummy looking yellow concoction were pushed to Artimus, and he handed one to me first. The pineapple wedge and cherries told me to expect something fruity. Taking a sip, I found I was right, and the drink was delicious. "Yum."

The way Artimus's lips pulled up to one side made me laugh. He picked up his drink then took my hand again, leading me out to dance. The multitude of bodies forced ours close together, moving to the music's steady beat.

This wasn't the kind of dancing we'd done at the charity function. This was the type of dancing where people would grind their bodies against each other. The type of dancing that led to other things.

I'd had no idea what I'd signed myself up for when I'd taken him up on this invitation. The drink was too good, and I couldn't taste a bit of alcohol in it. That made it easy to drink, and I did so a bit too fast.

When my glass was empty, I found a table nearby and left it there. Artimus put his down too, even though it wasn't finished. He took me into his arms, moving his body against mine.

I wrapped my arms around his neck, letting the music move me the way it wanted to. A few flashes of light caught our attention and we looked toward the source. Some man was taking pictures, and took a few more of us before moving on.

Normally, I'd be kind of mad that someone would have the nerve to do something so rude. But I wasn't acting like my normal self. No, I was acting like a woman who didn't have a care in the world.

Artimus's lips touched the shell of my ear. "We'll probably make the papers and be all over social media again tomorrow."

I nodded in agreement but just couldn't find it in me to care. Our faces were so close. His breath was warm on my skin as he held me with a loose grip, looking into my eyes.

Just do it.

At that moment I wanted Artimus to let his animal side out. I wanted him to take me and make me his. I didn't care who saw him do it, either.

"Are you feeling okay, Julia?" His dark brows furrowed, his eyes concerned.

"I'm just fine, Artimus." My words slurred together.

Why's that happening?

"We have to go." He released me from his embrace to take my hand, leading me out of the crowd.

"No," I protested.

It didn't stop him though. He led me all the way out of the club and straight into his waiting car.

"Hey, how did this get here so fast?" I mumbled as Artimus put me into the car.

I watched as he rolled his eyes. "The same way as always. I texted the driver that we were leaving and he came to pick us up. I can't believe that one drink has hit you so hard."

I ran my hands through my hair. "So soft. So silky."

Artimus put my seatbelt on for me, and I grabbed his face as his body moved back by me. "Julia, what are you doing?"

"Why don't you just kiss me, Arty?" I hiccupped. "Ha! Arty. Has anyone ever called you that?"

"Yes, my old assistant called me that. I can't say I like it coming from you." He pulled away from me. "Now let's get you home."

"Home?" I shook my head, and the movement made me dizzy. I held out my arms to steady myself because I felt as if I might fall right off the seat. "Whoa!"

Artimus put one arm around me then pushed my head to rest on his big shoulder. "Here, just rest. You'll feel better in the morning."

"I feel better now, Arty." I hiccupped again. "Do you know what word rhymes with Arty?" I put my finger to my lips. "Shh. Don't say it. Let me. Farty. Ha! Arty Farty, Farty Arty. Ha!" Even in my inebriated state, I wished that my laughter could have come out in sweeter, more feminine giggles, instead of the obnoxious squawks that I didn't seem able to control.

"You're a real riot, Julia." He stroked my hair, putting an end to my laughter at my clever joke. "You just rest that funny little brain of yours now."

I threw one leg over his leg and moved my hand up and down his chest, which was covered with a black button-down shirt. For some reason, I didn't like that those buttons were buttoned up. I began to fix that, but only got one undone before he took me by the wrist.

"No, no, Julia." He kissed my hand then held it against his chest. "Rest now."

I didn't want to rest. I wanted to play.

I didn't understand him. I was ready. Why wasn't he ready?

Pulling my head off his shoulder, which I didn't realize would make my head feel so heavy, I slurred, "Okay, Arty. I'm ready for you now. I am. I don't care that you won't tell me what I want to hear."

He placed his finger to my lips. "Julia, just stop."

I didn't stop though. I kept on talking even with his finger on my lips. "No ... I want you ... I. Want. You. Now."

Pulling his finger away from my lips, he looked closely at me then rolled down the window to talk to the driver. "Take us back to my penthouse."

"Yes, sir," came the driver's reply. "Home it is."

Wet heat pooled between my legs. Artimus was going to let his animal take control of both of us. Just like in my fantasies. And I was ready for that to happen.

As the window went back up, I struggled to climb onto his lap and get the first kiss out of the way. But something was pinning me to the seat. Then Artimus put a halt to my struggling as he held me tightly to his side. He kept shushing me as he ran his hand through my hair. "You just relax. We'll be home soon, Julia."

It was useless to struggle. My energy was running low anyway, and I didn't want to burn it all up before I got to experience Artimus in all his glory.

There wasn't any need to do anything anyway. We would go

home, he would take my clothes off, then his, and I'd get to see him naked.

The thought thrilled me, sending a shiver through me. "Artimus, don't be gentle with me just because it's my first time. I want you to be how you always are. Take me like an animal."

"Hush now." He began to hum now as he continued to stroke my hair.

His body vibrated with the tune he was humming, and I began to feel sleepy. When a yawn came out of me, I whimpered, "I might fall asleep. You wake me up when we get to your place. Promise me."

"Hush," came his one-word reply.

What happened after that was a little hazy. When I opened my eyes, the sun streamed through the windows of a bedroom. A bedroom I was all alone in.

Pushing the blanket back, I saw that I still had on the red silk bra and panty set I'd put on underneath the black dress, but nothing else.

Sitting up, my head pounded, and I quickly lay back down as a groan escaped me. "What the hell happened to me?"

Flashes of Artimus and me sitting in the back of his car began to flash through my mind. He and I were sitting close together. He was stroking my hair. I was telling him that I wanted him to take me like an animal.

I pulled the blanket up to cover my head. "Don't tell me that I really said that to him."

Moving my ass a bit, I noticed there wasn't any stiffness or pain in my lower region at all. "Thank God. He didn't do what I asked him to."

But even as I said that, a thought hit me.

He didn't do what I had asked him to!

Did he not want me? Had my little adventure into accidental drunkenness turned him off? Was it that easy for him to flip the switch on how he felt about me?

CHAPTER TWENTY-SIX

Artimus

The noon hour came and Julia still hadn't come out of the bedroom. I knocked on the door softly. "Julia?" I heard her groan, letting me know she was awake. "Can I come in? I've got aspirin and coffee."

When it came, her voice was more like a growl. "K."

Opening the door, I found her holding the covers tightly to her chest. Her cheeks were bright red, and I wasn't sure if it was caused by embarrassment, or the after-effects of the alcohol. "Did you undress me?"

"Of course not." I had to laugh. "Is that why you've been hiding out in here?"

She nodded then held her hand to one side of her head. "Yeah. Well, that, and I've got a monster hangover."

Monster hangover or not, the woman was still beautiful. Her hair hung in a mess around her shoulders, her makeup smudged beyond belief. Red lipstick only covered half of her mouth. She reminded me of Harley Quinn, that sexy female character from The Suicide Squad.

I went over to her, offering her the ibuprofen. "And with only one drink too. Here, take these. I had the night maid take your clothes off. I'd never disrespect you like that, Julia. You should know that by now." I put the mug of coffee I'd brought on the nightstand, picking up the bottle of water I'd had the maid leave with her the night before. "Here you go. Drink this."

Julia had passed out in the car. I'd carried her inside, which the doorman was classy enough to ignore. Bringing her into my apartment, I took her to the guest room across the hall from my bedroom, leaving her on the bed. I asked the maid to see to her and make sure she was comfortable then gave her the bottle of water, instructing her to place it on the nightstand.

Unlike the other night Julia had spent at my home, I didn't have any problem at all going to sleep. I knew there was no way I would touch her in that condition.

She popped the two pills into her mouth then took a drink of water. "Thank you, Artimus."

"No Arty Farty today, Julia?" I smoothed her hair as she winced at the reminder. Not one to make fun of anyone, I decided that was enough teasing. "Take a shower. I've already got clothes coming for you to change into before you go home. Unless you'd like to do something together today?"

"I should go home." She rubbed one eye with the back of her hand, further smearing the black mascara. "It's not that I wouldn't like to do something with you today, but things are getting a little harder for me since we're spending so much time out of work together. I hope you understand and aren't offended."

I wasn't offended. As a matter of fact, I had been thinking along those same lines. I hadn't realized just how on-edge Julia was until the night before. Whatever I'd had planned no longer seemed right.

"I am disappointed, but I understand. And I even agree. Things are getting harder for me too. I couldn't take my eyes off you last night. And the fact is, I'm having a hell of a time keeping my hands off you right now." I ran my hand up and down her bare arm, my cock pulsing as I did so.

Julia had an idea of how she wanted to live her life. One man, one true love. That was at the core of her idea. I couldn't be that for her right then. I wouldn't subject her to anymore trickery to get her to give me a chance without giving her the commitment she wanted.

When she was so eager last night, even though I knew it was the alcohol talking, I knew I had an advantage other men didn't have with her. She was attracted to me. Felt a connection to me—hell, she even thought that I was the one. And I had had plans to use that advantage to my benefit, ignoring what her dream had always been.

I had thought that if she could just feel the intensity of the attraction between us, then she wouldn't care so much about the commitment. But I understood now what she'd meant before. If she gave in before she was ready—no matter how attracted to me she was—then she could come to regret her decision. Or even worse, she could come to resent me.

Maybe I wasn't the right man for her since I couldn't give her what she deserved. She deserved a man who knew what he wanted without a shadow of a doubt. A man who would freely give himself to her without any limitations. She was smart enough to know that that was exactly what she deserved, and I had been too consumed by lust to see it for myself.

Her red-rimmed eyes sparkled as she looked at me. "I want you to know that I really respect you, Artimus. You've been very understanding about what I want, and you aren't trying to push me into anything just so you can get what you want. That's commendable." Her eyes shifted to one side, her cheeks going ruby red. "I've gotten little glimpses of what I did last night. A lesser man would've taken advantage of that." She looked back at me with a smile on her face. "Thank you for being the good man you are, and for not doing what I asked you to last night. And I'm sorry I put you in that situation—that it might seem like I'm sending you mixed messages."

Rubbing her shoulder, I was finding it harder and harder to stop myself from touching her. Her skin made mine blaze in a way that defied imagination. "It wasn't hard at all to do the right thing. I want to make you a promise right here, right now. If I can't give you what you want, then I won't ask for a thing from you." I'd put it all out there for her. I wouldn't be playing any games. She was the type of woman who didn't mess around with all those games people played. I wasn't above them yet. I knew that.

I might not ever be.

Julia was special. She deserved someone just as special as she was.

She looked kind of sad, her eyes downcast. "I'm sorry I'm not normal, Artimus."

Taking her by the chin, I lifted her pretty face up to make her look into my eyes. "I'm glad you're not normal. You're perfect just as you are. You're a shining star, Julia Bengal. Don't apologize for that. I'm the one who's sorry. I wish I had it in me to believe the way you do. Unfortunately, life has left me a little jaded. You're smart to live the way you have, waiting for the right man to come along. It's my own past with women that makes me doubt that the forever love you talk about is real."

Nodding in understanding, she whispered, "Artimus, I wish I could show you my thoughts. I wish I could make you see what I see. If you could see what I do, then I doubt you would have any problem devoting yourself to me the way I know I could devote myself to you."

I had to know what she saw. "What is it that you see, Julia?"

Shaking her head, she answered, "It's not easy to explain. There are lots of feelings. Tons of sensations. This knowledge that you are the man for me. Call it an instinct, I don't know how else to describe it. The only thing missing is the part where you believe the same way I do." Her eyes shimmered as she looked at me. "Am I crazy, Artimus? Have I allowed myself to believe in something that can never be real?"

Had she?

I took a moment to digest what she'd said. She felt things on a much deeper level than I ever had. "The way you talk about how you feel sounds like a fairytale."

A deep sigh made her chest heave. "That's what Nina and Lila have told me too. My expectations are too high. No one can meet them." She let the blanket fall away from her bra-covered breasts. Taking my hand, she pulled it to her heart. I could feel it beating just beneath the surface, between her beautiful breasts. "Should I abandon my beliefs for you, Artimus? Should I put faith in you and just hope that you'll give me forever in the end? If you think so, then I will do that. I'll do it because I trust you. I trust you more than anyone I've ever known."

There it was. All I had to do was tell her that she should trust me, and we could be together like a regular couple. Julia was willing to let her rules and stipulations slide a little, but only for me.

If she had that kind of faith that we were meant to be together, then why couldn't I find that faith too?

"Give me more time, Julia." I kissed her cheek. "I don't want you to give up your dream. Trust me when I tell you that, at this time, I'm not the man you want. I want you in a way I've never wanted anyone. Don't think for one second that I don't. But I want to be the man you deserve. The man you've dreamt about your whole life. Give me time to find that man. He has to be in here somewhere, right? After all, you can see him clearly. I want to find him too. It's what you deserve, Julia."

She laughed lightly as she let my hand go. "And that's why I trust you so much, Artimus. Your actions are always commendable."

"As commendable as my actions are, I'm no saint. I'll get out of here before I do something that I can't take back." My fingertips grazed her cheek. "My lips ache to kiss yours. My body is angry with me for not taking advantage of your offer. But I can fight those urges to give you what you need."

Her smile faded as she watched me get up. "I'll see you tomorrow at work then. I hope you have a good day."

"You too, Julia." Words filled my head, trying to come out of my mouth. But I wouldn't let them until I was sure. I left the room, only to fall back against the door.

How did I get in so deep? When did this happen to me?

My brain was buzzing with the exact words I knew she wanted to hear. *I love you.* The urge to say them out loud kept me biting tongue. I fought myself not to open that door back up and say them to her.

I felt like my body and my brain were at war. My body was using everything in its arsenal to get what it wanted—Julia, underneath it. I wouldn't give it what it wanted. Not until I could tell her that I loved her and that I was ready to give her forever.

My heart ached because I wanted her so badly. Part of me wished she had more standard ideas about sex and dating, but the other part of me knew she wouldn't be so damn perfect if she wasn't exactly the way she was.

I had to drag my feet to my bedroom. All they wanted to do was take me back to her. She had said she trusted me and would do whatever I wanted.

I planted my ass in a chair. She didn't know it, but she had put herself in a precarious position. The primitive man inside of me was putting up one hell of a fight against the man she must imagine me to be. The one I wanted to be for her.

I felt pushed and pulled in every direction. Julia wasn't truly safe until she was out from under my roof. I prayed that she could find the conviction she had shown me every day since today. Because I knew that without it, she was in danger of losing the dream she had held onto for so many years.

Going into the bathroom, I took off every stitch of clothing I had before hopping into the shower. I had to take my mind off the woman across the hallway. I had to pretend she wasn't anywhere near me.

My fist pumped my cock with a savageness it never had before. I growled, feeling like something was clawing its way through my body. There was something inside of me that wanted Julia with a desperation that bordered on obsession. Something wild, untamed, and unknown.

I'd heard people talking about finding their soulmate. Not all of them knew it right away, but somehow they figured it out. Was that what this was?

All I knew for certain was that I had never felt anything like this in my life. There was a part of me that demanded her. It was powerful. It was forceful. And it wanted to be set free so it could be with the one person in the entire universe who was meant for him.

How long could I keep him buried inside?

CHAPTER TWENTY-SEVEN

Julia

L ater that evening, when the hangover had worn off, I took advantage of the free time I had and decided to simply relax. Bethey was at work and wouldn't be back until late—she had an article that had to be in before midnight, and the reporter she worked under had kept her at the office to make sure it got done.

Lying on the sofa, shuffling through Facebook on my cell, I jumped when it rang. *Mom* appeared on my screen, so I answered. "Hey, Mom."

"Hey, yourself, Julia Bengal. You haven't called me in nine days. That's two days longer than you've ever waited to call home. So what gives?"

I hadn't realized that many days had gone by since I'd talked to her. "Sorry, Mom. My head has been in the clouds. Something has happened."

"Like what?"

Unsure whether or not I should tell her anything about Artimus, I thought I probably should. If he ever did come around, then I would have to introduce them anyway. "I've fallen in love, Mom."

She didn't say anything for a moment. When she did, she sounded cynical. "With who?"

"Artimus Wolfe." The sound of his name hung in the air. My insides felt as if hundreds of tiny fairies were sprinkling their magic dust around everywhere, just at the mention of his name.

Then her shrill voice pulled me out of my wonderful little moment. "Your boss?"

Yeah, she's not going to take it well.

"Technically, yes. But he's so much more than that, and always has been, really." I had to sit up, taking a more formal stance so I could make a proper argument. "He's so great, Mom. Like you have no idea how great he is."

"Oh, I've got some kind of idea about the man, Julia." The sound of her swatting something told me she was chasing the cat out of the house again. The old tabby cat loved to be inside, but she couldn't stop herself from clawing up the sofa.

"And what kind of idea do you have, Mom?" I asked with a sarcastic tone.

"The idea that he's taking advantage of you and you'll come home after losing this great job you've managed to get. You don't understand this about yourself, and I suppose it's my fault for letting it go on too long. Frankly, it kept you from becoming a problem as a teenager, so your father and I were more than happy when you kept up your story about soulmates and finding 'the one.' It gave us no reason to worry about you."

It bothered me that she thought she and Dad had anything to do with the way I thought. "So, what is this thing that I don't understand about myself, Mom?"

"You don't understand that you've made it impossible for any man to live up to your standards. When this guy falls short of your grand expectations, this will be over. You and he will end, and so will your job. Can't you see that?" The sound of the screen door slamming let me know she'd chased the cat outside.

Is she right?

But it wasn't just her, was it? She was the fourth person to tell me that I had set my expectations too high for any mere mortal man to live up to. Could they all be wrong?

I have to be fooling myself.

"Mom, do you think I'm capable of changing the way I think?" I had to know if the one person who knew me best thought I was capable of changing in this.

"No." She made my heart spin out of control with that one word.

"No?" I nearly cried.

"Not without some serious heartbreak, Julia. Or some therapy." She sighed, and I knew she felt responsible. "This is my fault. I read you tons of fairytales when you were little. Prince Charming always showed up, and he and the princess would know in an instant that they had found their perfect match. But those are just stories, Julia."

I fell back on the sofa, covering my eyes with my arm. "Mom, what I see, what I think, isn't like those stories you read to me. I don't need a hero. I am not a damsel in distress. I just want to find the one man who was meant for me. And I know you think I'm crazy, or that my expectation are too high, but I've found him. I know I have."

"And have you told him how you feel—about him and about relationships in general?" she asked with skepticism.

"I have," I said boldly.

"Okay. So, has he confessed his undying love for you and told you that he knows you're the one for him too, the way you've always said would happen?" Now she'd done it. She was throwing my old words back in my face.

I sat up, new determination sparking my ire. "I was a kid back then, Mom. I didn't know how life worked back then. I'm an adult now. And Artimus has told me that life has jaded him somewhat. He's not yet the man he needs to be for me. He needs time."

"Time," she said with a huff. "For what, baby girl? To figure out how to let you down without bruising your ego? Time to look for a new assistant, since the one he has is a little on the loopy side?"

I stopped breathing as I processed what she said. My mother had called me crazy. She'd never done that before.

Am I crazy?

"Whatever happened to Price Stone?" she asked me. "Now that guy had his head on straight. He let you know how it really is. I suppose you didn't like him doing that. But he was right, Julia. Expecting the perfect connection and the perfect relationship right from the get-go is silly and impractical. Relationships take time, and you're throwing away good men just because you don't feel like magical connection with them right at the first glance. Don't be mad at Price and shut him out just because he had the balls to be truthful with you. This Artimus fella would do better by you if he was more like Price."

She was wrong about Price, but I didn't want to get into it with her about that. "Do you really think that Artimus is just placating me?"

She laughed. "He has to be, darling. Think about it. Not everyone —and especially not some fancy New York billionaire, I'd bet—is ready to promise their life away before testing the physical relations waters a bit first. There might be some men out there who would be okay with that, but I've yet to meet one."

I thought there had to be lots of people who would do that. In other cultures, things like that happened all the time. In some countries, divorce wasn't even allowed.

But did that mean that their marriages were happy?

I had no idea what that answer was.

Maybe Mom was right. Maybe I had lived in a fantasy world a little bit.

"I told Artimus that I trusted him." I ran my hand up and down my arm, which had goosebumps all over it remembering that intense moment. "I told him that we could have a relationship without him promising me forever."

She hummed a little before saying, "And yet he didn't jump on that, did he?"

No, he hadn't jumped on it. And I had found that admirable at the time.

But maybe he hadn't jumped on that because he had already lost interest.

I felt lost. "Mom, what can I do?"

"Just do your job. Lay off the love stuff. If you don't say anything about it, then he might not either. He sounds as if he's non-confrontational. That can be a good thing. That means there's a very good chance that he'll let this thing blow over and you will get to keep your job."

Can I do that?

My mouth opened, and my words poured out before I could hold them back. "Mom, I love him though." My eyes filled with tears. "I can't just pretend nothing happened."

"Well, you better." She clucked her tongue. "If you don't, then you can count yourself unemployed very soon. Mark my words."

I hated when she said that. She'd never been wrong after saying those three words.

Mom was very perceptive and had great intuition, so she just seemed to have a way of knowing things. I had to give her that. But how much could she really know about what Artimus thought and what he would do?

She didn't know the man at all.

"Mom, I feel kind of sick. I should get off the phone. I think I'll take a long bath with a bottle of wine and try to pull my head out of my ass. Apparently, it has been stuck up there for my whole life."

"I love you, baby girl. And I am sorry for letting this thing go on far too long. I had high hopes that Price Stone would set you straight so then I wouldn't have to."

"Love you too, bye." I ended the call, not feeling good about anything.

I was a looney bird. I had never felt so ridiculous, so dumb. And I had no idea how I could make Artimus see me as anything other than a nut-job when even my own mother was calling me crazy.

Getting up, I went to the kitchen to pick out a bottle of wine to help drown my sorrows. On the counter, I saw Bethey's house keys. She'd left them behind again.

After opening a bottle of red, I went to unlock the door. After the bath, I would be heading to bed and didn't want to be woken up when she came home.

I shot Bethey a text, letting her know her keys were home and I'd left the door unlocked, and that I was going to go to bed early. She sent back a *thank you,* then I went to fill up the tub with hot soapy water, hoping it would help wash my craziness away.

It was obviously time to at least loosen up on my naive dream of having just one man for me; if not let it go entirely. I was tired of people thinking I was crazy. I didn't think my vision for the future would go away entirely—I would never stop thinking I deserved the love of a committed man—but maybe I had to learn how to hide it. And maybe I could loosen up my rules on physical intimacy just a little.

But the thought of engaging in any kind of sexual activity with anyone other than Artimus made me shudder—and not in a good way.

So maybe my future wouldn't include the man I thought was made just for me. But I might find someone I could at least stand to be around.

Going back the kitchen, I poured myself a glass of wine, filling it to the tippy top, then going to the bathroom to strip down and settle into what I prayed, by some miracle, would be healing water.

If there were any miracles.

Perhaps those weren't real either.

My cell rang so I looked at it, as I'd placed it within reach on the vanity. Price's name was on the screen. I didn't answer it, letting it go to voicemail. But my eyes couldn't seem to leave the phone.

I knew I needed to let Artimus know that I was dropping this whole thing. It would make the next day, when we were at work, easier.

It would be too hard to say the words, so I texted them.

Artimus, I'm sorry. You must think I'm crazy. And you're probably right. I must be. I am taking this whole thing off the table. I don't want you to worry about me bringing up anything about us or how we were meant to be together ever again. I think it's time I let go of these childish ideas about love and romance, and I'm sorry I involved you in my silly fantasies. Please feel free to act

normal at work. I'll try my best to do that too. If we can't find a way to put my craziness behind us, then I will resign.

I read over the words ten times before I sent that text. Then I turned my cell off. I didn't want to talk to anyone else today. I needed time to focus on getting my head right, taking it out of the clouds and grounding myself in reality for once in my life.

Tomorrow will be the first day of my life as a normal person who is more open-minded about love, and who doesn't think that one man, one woman, forever entangled in body and soul, is the only relationship worth having.

CHAPTER TWENTY-EIGHT

Artimus

I read her text twenty times before I could really believe she'd written it.

Julia Bengal had brought things out in me that I didn't know existed. Her belief in something so extraordinary had just begun to seep into my mind. I'd been able to look into my future so many times since I'd met her, and it all revolved around her. So how could she be telling me that she was just crazy and that the future I had been planning for us would never happen?

Julia had a spirit about her that I had never witnessed before. Everything about her pulled me to her, and yet here she was, saying that she must be crazy.

Crazy for what? Believing in a love that could withstand time? Or just believing in love, period? Believing there was only one man for her and that I was that man?

If she was crazy, then I was crazy too.

The craziest thing about this was the 180 she'd pulled, going from promising me everything just that morning to saying she didn't want anything anymore.

Someone must've told her that she was nuts for revealing her dreams and her feelings to me. Someone had to have told her that when I didn't jump at the chance to take her, that meant I didn't really want her.

That feeling nagged at me for a while before I decided I had to call her. But when I did, the call went straight to voicemail. That had me thinking that she'd blocked my number out of sheer embarrassment.

That wouldn't stop me though, so I went to find the nearest member of my staff and found one of the maids. I used her phone to call Julia, and that call went right to voicemail too.

"She has the phone turned off, sir," the maid informed me as she took her cell phone back and put it in her apron pocket.

"You're right, I'm sure." I headed back to my bedroom to think about what I should do.

It was nine at night. Not so late that she would be asleep. We did need to talk about things. I wasn't willing to let her go. Especially after one single text message.

But was I willing to bet on us? I didn't want to promise her something that I knew deep down she still wanted—no matter what that message said—and then end up disappointing her. If I was going to chase after her, I had to make sure I was ready for that huge commitment.

I had no idea what exactly was stopping me from giving into my feelings for her. Fear of what? Love? Passion? Honesty?

Falling back on my bed, I lay there looking at the ceiling. And that was where I found the answer.

Julia Bengal is too good to be true.

That was it, wrapped in a nutshell. Julia wasn't normal. She was beyond compare. Intensely fresh and eager, all the while being subtle and classic. There was no one else like her in the world; I was sure of that.

And she wants me.

So why was I lying on my bed instead of getting my ass up and getting to her as fast as I could? I had to let her know that I wasn't afraid anymore.

Then I realized why I was lying there, not moving a muscle. I needed to get a ring. I needed to make arrangements for us to get married as soon as possible. Because if I went to her with a proclamation of love and forever, I still wouldn't be able to have her fully until I was married to her.

Or at least that's what I assumed she wanted.

Her spirituality was still a bit of a mystery to me. Was her idea of being together conventional? Or was it unconventional?

Would simply being together be enough?

Again, I had no idea, and all that told me was that we didn't know each other well enough to make such a huge decision like marriage just yet. And even as I thought that, my heart pumped harder in my chest, and I swore it screamed the word *coward* at me.

I smacked myself in the chest. "I am not a coward."

Yes, you are, my heart pulsed back at me.

I had no idea a person could have a conversation with their own heart. But there I was, doing just that.

"Would a coward take the risks I have taken? Would a coward take on setting up a new network, using entirely new faces to man that network? I think not." I pounded my chest the way Tarzan would. "I am not a coward."

And my heart replied, *Then take this risk. Give yourself entirely to that woman, and in return, she will give herself entirely to you. Have your happily ever after, Arty Farty.*

I couldn't believe my own heart would stoop to calling me names.

So, I got up off my bed, walked to my closet to get changed, and headed out to get my driver to take me to Julia.

I read that text all the way to her apartment building. When we stopped, I got out and went inside. It wasn't until the elevator ride that I started to get worried.

What if she really thinks she's crazy now? What if she really has given up on everything? What if I can't get her to believe that I want her just the way she was—rules and conditions, dreams and all?

The elevator stopped on her floor and I got out. As I got to her door, I noticed that it had been left ajar. "Is she crazy? This is New York. No one leaves their doors partially open." I walked in and closed and locked the door behind me. "Julia?"

There wasn't a single light on in the apartment. I felt along the wall and finally found the light switch. It turned on a small lamp that sat on an end table at the other end of the sofa. But it gave me enough light to find my way to the small hallway that had three doors off it. The one in the middle, I assumed, was the bathroom door. So, one of the other two had to be Julia's.

I heard a muffled sound coming from the room on the right. A deep voice came from that one too.

Was that her roommate's bedroom? Did her roomie have a man over?

I opted not to open that one first and opened the door on the left. It wasn't locked, so I pushed the door open and found a mound on top of the bed. "Julia?" I whispered.

When there was no reply, I made my way to the bed and touched the lump, feeling that it was too squishy to be a human. I turned on the bedside lamp and found out it wasn't a person at all but a pile of laundry.

So, the other bedroom had to be Julia's.

I felt a thud as my heart dropped, knowing that that was the room I had heard the male voice coming from.

If she was with someone, I had to know. Maybe Julia really was too good to be true. Maybe her wonderful personality was just an act. I had to know, one way or the other.

Quietly, I went back to that door, leaning on it and putting my ear against the door, trying to hear anything I could. And I did hear things. What I heard made chills flow through me and had my stomach tied up in knots.

"You whore, you know you want my fat cock buried deep in your pussy." The sound of something smacking against flesh could be heard, and I couldn't take anymore.

I threw the door open. "No!" I gasped at what I'd found.

Price Stone, wearing only a tight black pair of underwear, spun around to look at me. "What do you want?" he slurred, clearly drunk.

In his hand was a leather belt. And across Julia's exposed left ass cheek was a long, raised welt. She was lying, face down, on the bed. Dark blue silk panties covered her. An oversized T-shirt, which she must've put on to go to sleep in, had been ripped open. Only shreds of white material covered parts of her torso. Her back had several red lash marks on it.

Wide eyes full of fear looked at me over her mouth, which had been stuffed with a ball-gag. Her hands were tied behind her back. Her ankles were tied to the bedposts, spreading her legs apart.

Price stumbled as he tried to stand up to me. "I'm not sharing, Wolfe. Get the fuck out of here."

I had no idea if Julia was into this shit or not. How could she go from telling me she was a virgin, to this? Something didn't seem right. "Julia, do you want this?"

Price looked back at her. "You shut your fucking mouth, you slut." He raised the belt and made an attempt to hit her with it again.

My hand stopped him, catching his wrist before he hit her tender flesh again. "You will not hit her while I'm here, Price. Now I want to know exactly what's going on." I shoved him back, moving to take the gag out of Julia's mouth so she could tell me what was happening.

But I didn't make it to her before Price slammed something down on the back of my head. I fell to the floor, cursing as I went. "You fucking dick!"

Price was right there, holding a wooden chair up high over his head. "Get out of here. I'm going to take what's mine, and there's nothing you can do about it. I told her I would kill you if you tried to stop me, Artimus Wolfe. And I will do it too. I've put enough of my time into this prick tease. I've put myself out over this bitch. I will not lose what's rightfully mine. I get her virginity, then you can have the bitch. I always get what I want, and I want that from her. I've earned it."

"You're insane, Price." I put my hand on the bed to pull myself up, but he hit me with the chair again. This time stars filled my vision. I had never been hit so hard.

His foot connected with my ribs, knocking the air out of my lungs. I fell to my side in a breathless heap. Darkness was coming in from all sides of my vision.

I could hear Julia screaming and whimpering behind the gag.

She needed me, and I was lying helplessly on the floor, unable to do a damn thing. Price was a madman who was about to take the one thing she'd guarded her whole life.

His voice sounded evil as he growled, "Julia, prepare yourself, my little kumquat."

The sound of material ripping followed by Julia's muffled screams filled my ears and broke my heart into a million pieces. "Don't," I managed to get out. The air was finally coming back into my lungs.

"Shut the fuck up!" Price shouted, then I felt him kick me in the back three times. "I'm going to fuck this bitch, then she's all yours, Moneybags."

Pain radiated all through my body from the spot he'd kicked. It traveled up my spine, through my neck before going all over my head. I had no idea what was happening to me.

Am I about to die?

CHAPTER TWENTY-NINE

Julia

After finishing the entire glass of wine while soaking in the hot bath, I felt a little dizzy and lightheaded. My eyelids were heavy, and I felt confident that I should be able to fall asleep pretty quickly.

I dried off then wrapped my robe around me before going to my bedroom to dress for bed and climb under the blankets. Pulling on a fresh pair of panties, I then got a big white T-shirt out of my drawer and put it on. Walking past my full-length mirror, I noticed I could see my dark blue panties underneath the white material.

It wasn't like it mattered; no one would be seeing me like that anyway. I shrugged then went to get into my bed.

A sound in the living room made me pause on the edge of my bed. I went to the bedroom door to tell Bethey goodnight. But when I pulled my door open, Price was in the hallway, looking at me.

My first instinct was to close my door, which I tried to do, but his body was right there in no time, stopping me from doing that. "No!"

"Yes," he snarled at me.

I was no match for the muscular man. Somehow, he turned me

around and had my hands tied in an instant. He pushed me face down on the bed then pulled one of my legs to one side, tying it to the bedpost.

I kicked with my free leg while trying my best to move my arms to loosen the rope that bound my wrists. "Stop!" I screamed at the top of my lungs.

For a moment I thought he'd come to his senses. He was obviously drunk. I could smell the alcohol coming off him in waves. But then I realized he wasn't stopping at all as he placed a ball in my mouth, gagging me then tying a strap around my head to keep it there.

I tried to scream again, but only a muffled sound came out. No one would hear me now. And that told me that he had planned this shit out. He hadn't been drunk when he got the rope to tie me up, or when he'd bought the gag to silence me.

Price Stone had been planning to do this to me. I wondered just how long he'd been biding his time, making this up in his head. And I wondered if I could stop him.

With my screams effectively muffled, he got back to his task, tying my other ankle to the other bedpost, spreading me out. At least I still had my shirt and panties on.

Something cold moved over the skin on my back, and then I heard the sound of material being ripped. I could feel my T-shirt falling in strands of fabric on my back and sides. He was cutting it with what felt like a knife.

That was when I began to cry. I knew what was about to happen, and he'd made sure that I was too defenseless to stop him.

His lips pressed against my ear. "I'm going to take what's mine, Julia. I'm done waiting. I'm done begging. I am done saying that I'm sorry for what I did to you. I'm not sorry. I'm only sorry that you got away from me that night before I could do to you then what I'm doing now."

He laughed cruelly as he loosened the gag to let me speak. "You won't get away with this, Price. Don't do this. Artimus will kill you if you hurt me."

"Artimus? You mean your boss? You mean the man you've claimed you're not dating? But the pictures in the paper this morning tell another story completely. I saw you two grinding on each other when I opened the paper this morning. Imagine how upset I was. So, has he already taken what's rightfully mine? Or have you held him off the way you've done so many others, you little cunt?"

I wasn't sure what to say. If I told him I wasn't a virgin anymore, it might dampen his lust for me. "Yes, he and I have fucked nine ways to Sunday. You're too late for that, Price."

He made a terrible growling noise then fire ripped through me as something came crashing down on my back. "Liar!"

"Price!" I cried out. "Artimus will kill you."

He hurried to put the gag back into my mouth and made it even tighter when he tied it up to hold it in place. "If he tries to stop me, I will kill him, Julia. Mark my words." I felt the belt running over my back. "Each time you lie to me about your virginity, I will strike you. Do you understand me?"

I nodded.

"Good." He leaned in close, his stinking breath making me sick. "Are you still a virgin?"

I shook my head, still thinking he wouldn't want me if he thought otherwise. I could take a beating. I didn't think I could take the other thing he had in mind.

Another strike set my flesh on fire, and then he asked me the same question again. Again, I shook my head. Another strike made me feel like I was about to throw up.

I couldn't take anymore. With that gag in my mouth, I would choke, possibly to death, if I threw up.

"Julia, are you still a virgin?" came his question.

With tears streaming from my eyes, I nodded, knowing I was done for.

He stood beside me so I could see what he was doing as he started taking his clothes off. He stripped down until he was wearing only a pair of tight black underwear that hugged his body. The bulge at his cock drew my attention. It wasn't that big; maybe it wouldn't hurt too badly.

I could just zone out. I could go somewhere else, in my head. Maybe then it wouldn't scar me for life.

He moved out of my line of sight, and I felt the belt hit my ass. I screamed again, only a muffle coming out. Then I heard my bedroom door open.

Artimus's voice rang out. "No!"

Thank God!

Price was so drunk he seemed almost unfazed as he asked in slurred words, "What do you want?" There was a pause before he went on. "I'm not sharing, Wolfe. Get the fuck out of here."

"Julia, do you want this?" he asked me, his confusion clear.

Before I could shake my head to let him know that I was definitely not into this, Price interrupted. "You shut your fucking mouth, you slut," he shouted. I heard the belt as he pulled it back through the air, preparing to hit me with it again. I clenched my ass cheeks in anticipation of the pain.

The rest of what happened past in a blur. I tried to pay attention to what was happening as I heard what clearly sounded to me as feet and other objects connecting with bone and muscle. I couldn't see who had the upper hand, as they were fighting just out of my line of vision.

I had thought I couldn't be more terrified than I had been a few moments ago, but the thought that Artemis was now in the same room with a man who was determined to kill him shook me to my very core. I could hardly follow along with their conversation as panic tore through me at the thought of Artimus being murdered in front of me.

"You're insane, Price." I could finally feel Artimus trying to pull himself up, using the bed.

I closed my eyes, praying he could get up and deal with Price. The sound of a thud, then a harsh breath came from Artimus, and I was straining my eyes was again to see if I could see anything. I moved my head and saw out of the corner of my eye that Price was standing over Artimus as he lay on the floor, motionless.

All I could do was cry. Artimus was hurt. And I couldn't do a thing to help him. I felt so much guilt. If I had just told someone that Price had hit me before, then this might not be happening right now. Everything was my fault.

Price must've been satisfied that he'd taken Artimus out as he shifted his focus back to me. "Julia, prepare yourself, my little kumquat," he told me.

I felt my body being pulled up as Price grabbed my panties. They ripped right off me, leaving me bare-assed. My tears stopped as panic set in.

I've got to fight!

"Don't," Artimus moaned.

"Shut the fuck up!" Price shouted, and then I heard him kicking Artimus some more. "I'm going to fuck this bitch, then she's all yours, Moneybags."

Anger took over where panic had been. I pulled at the ropes that bound me. My arms, my legs, I pulled and pulled to get free of those damn ropes. I wasn't about to become Price Stone's victim.

I could feel Price's hands moving over my ass. "So pretty."

Then a tremendous roar filled the entire room, so loud and deep that made everything shake. Price's hands were no longer on my butt. I could hear his screams as he was tossed through the air. His head hit the wall near my headboard.

Price fell, hitting the floor hard. And then Artimus was there, picking him up and holding him while he punched him repeatedly in the face. Price was out cold; his body limp in Artimus' large hands.

I wiggled and whimpered, making Artimus stop his assault before he killed the man. Artimus looked at me, and then dropped Price to the floor.

His eyes lost the rage that had filled them seconds ago. They turned soft and caring as he looked at me. "Baby, everything is going to be okay now. You're safe."

I knew he was right. He was there. Everything was going to be okay.

He untied me, using the same ropes that had held me down to tie Price up, keeping him restrained so he couldn't do either of us any more harm while we waited for the police.

My robe was hanging on a hook on my closet door. Artimus went to get it, wrapping it around me. He sat on the bed beside me, holding my hand as I tried to stop crying.

"You okay?" he asked me as he ran his thumb over my cheek, brushing away the tears.

"No." I looked at him with a weak smile. "But I will be. Thanks to you."

"So he was the one who was harassing you, then," he said as he ran his hands through my hair to straighten it. "Wanna tell me what really happened between you two?"

"It was pretty normal at first. He didn't act crazy. I began to trust him. When he asked me to come to his apartment, I thought I would be safe. All our other dates were in public, and I would meet him places. That night at his apartment was the first and only time I was completely alone with him." I had to stop and take a deep breath, my heart racing at the memory.

Artimus ran his hand over my shoulder. "It's okay. Take your time, baby."

I took a few breaths, regaining my composure. "He was drunk when I got to his apartment. I should've just left right away, but I didn't. He continued to drink, and after a while he made me kiss him. Then he just went for it. He grabbed my boob, tried to put his hand down my pants. He told me he was going to fuck me, and I was going to like it. He told me to stop being a baby when I tried to get away from him. And then he hit me in the face."

Artimus looked back at the unconscious man on the floor. "I should just kill him right now."

I ran my hands around his neck and made him look at me instead. "No. He's not worth it. I did get away from him. I picked up a lamp and hit him in the head with it, knocking him out, and then I left. I should've gone straight to the police and pressed charges. I didn't, and that's why we're sitting here tonight." I couldn't hold back my tears any longer, running my fingers over the bruises on Artimus's lovely face before resting my head on his chest. "And now he's hurt you. This is all my fault, Artimus. I'm so sorry."

He pulled my head up, wiping away my tears as he shook his head. "This is not your fault. This is Price Stone's fault, and his alone. I never want you to blame yourself for what has happened to you. Promise me that, Julia."

I wasn't sure I could do that. For so long I had been blaming myself and feeling so ashamed, that I thought it might be impossible for me to think any other way. "I think I'm going to need help, Artimus."

"And you will get it." His hand cupped my chin, his thumb grazing over my lips. "And once you're healthy and ready mentally, then I want you to know that I'm ready."

I wasn't sure I understood him. "Ready for what?"

He moved off the bed and got down on both knees as he held my hands. "Julia Bengal, you are the one woman who was made for me. I give myself to you completely. You hold my heart and soul within you. I know that now. Julia, I am asking you to give me forever with you, if you still want forever with me."

I couldn't breathe or even think. But the words I had always known belonged to him came rushing out of my mouth, just as I had imagined they would someday. "Artimus Wolfe, you are the one man who was made just for me. You hold my heart and soul within you. I've waited for you for what seems like forever, and now we will have our forever. I am yours, Artimus, I always have been, and I always will be."

CHAPTER THIRTY

Artimus

After a few months of intense therapy, Julia was feeling much more herself, and was feeling mentally healthy for the first time since Price's attack. She had had her ups and downs, but she was constantly amazing me with her strength and resilience. And with Price in jail and soon heading to prison for the next fifty years, Julia had seen justice served.

I had waited patiently for her to get the help she needed to get back to the young woman she was before Price had broken into her home. We'd made our promises to one another but hadn't done anything more than that, other than spend most of our days together, just like we always had.

It was important to me that she really felt ready and okay after all that had happened to her. I didn't want to do anything to further traumatize her.

She'd stayed in her apartment with her roommate. I'd wanted her in my home, but she said she needed to learn how to feel safe on her own again before coming to live with me.

I did ask her about getting married, to which she responded that she didn't think that was necessary. Her exact words were, "Who needs a paper and a person to tell them what they already know?"

I had to agree with her. I would've married her in a heartbeat if she'd wanted that though. As it was, I had already made legal documents that would protect her financially if anything happened to me. She was my sole heir to everything I owned.

Julia claimed she didn't need any of that. But I had insisted on it. I wanted us to share everything, not just our lives and eventually our bodies.

The end of the workweek was at hand. On a Friday at 4:37 p.m., Julia came into my office. Her eyes were bright and shining. "I've got an idea for this weekend. Are you busy?"

"Nope." I leaned up in my chair, giving her my full attention. "What do you have in mind, Julia?"

She smiled shyly at me as she twirled a lock of her dark hair between her fingers. "I thought that I'd like to make the move this weekend. Start the more physical part of our union. If you're up for it, that is."

It took a moment for me to register what she was saying, but then it hit me. "You're ready to move in with me?"

She laughed and nodded. "And I'm ready for more too. I'm ready to be with you in every way, Artimus."

"We're going to have sex too?" I asked, as it was just kind of hard to believe that we were really going to add that in, finally.

She nodded. "Yeah. If you want. I'm ready if you are."

"Baby, you've got no idea how ready I am." I jumped up, picking her up bridal style. "We're going to spend the entire weekend and all of next week at our place in the Hamptons, baby."

She laughed as I carried her out through the lobby then into the elevator. "You seem excited."

"You better believe it." I kissed her then as we rode that elevator all the way down.

That was our first kiss.

I didn't feel our tongues touching, mingling with each other, though I know they did. What I did feel was hard to explain—it was more than mere physical sensation. I held her in my arms, but I didn't feel her there. I didn't feel my feet on the floor. I didn't notice the people who got on or off the elevator. All I noticed was how high I felt. As if she and I were floating far above the world.

She pulled her mouth away from mine. "We've stopped. Time to get off the elevator."

I put her down then took her by the hand. "Okay." I felt out of breath as we walked out to get into the car. The driver waited with the door open. "Um, home. Hers first. We're packing to go to the Hamptons for the week."

"Yes, sir," he said, and we went on our way.

Hours later we were at the mansion I'd told Julia about countless times, though she hadn't ever been to. "So, this is our home in the Hamptons, Julia. What do you think about it?"

Her eyes moved to look up the grand staircase. "I think it's lovely, but I would really like to see the master bedroom if you don't mind."

I didn't mind at all. Picking her up, I carried her up the stairs and to our bedroom. Laying her on the bed, I unzipped the dress she was wearing, which thankfully had a zipper running down the front of it. I shimmied it off her, leaving her in a pink bra and matching panties.

She smiled. "Now your turn." She got up on her knees, taking my shirt off then undoing my pants and pushing them to fall on the floor. "There, now we're both in our underwear."

"Not for long." I pulled her bra off then pushed her playfully back on the bed, then took her panties off too.

She crooked her finger at me, and I didn't think I'd ever been so hard in my life. "Come lie down so I can get rid of your underwear."

I did as she said and then we were finally both naked. She was on her knees, a vision of beauty with her creamy skin and dark hair flowing around her body.

She wiggled her finger again. "Come, get on your knees in front of me."

Moving to do whatever she said, I took her hands in mine, pulling them up to wrap around my neck before I placed mine on her hips. "I love you, Julia."

"And I love you, Artimus." She leaned in and our mouths met.

Warmth surrounded me instantly. The same floating effect occurred, and I felt like I wasn't in my body, yet I could feel every sensation that zipped through me. Lightning zigzagged around, followed my deep electric pulses. I felt more connected to her than I'd ever felt in all the months I'd known her.

I moved her to lie on her back, moving my body over hers. She spread her legs for me, her knees bent, and I could feel her feet on either side of my ass. My mouth left hers to kiss her entire body.

Her luscious tit filled my mouth. I bit her nipple, making her shriek. "Yes, more!"

She raked her nails across my back as I sucked her tit until I felt her body shivering. Only then did I leave it to kiss my way down the rest of her body.

Her hands tangled in my hair as I gently kissed her clit. I peppered it with soft kisses until it was swollen and three times the size it had been. I left it to lick my way through her hot folds, and then stabbed my tongue into her tight pussy.

"Yes, Artimus!" she gasped. She had no idea what was in store for her if she was this excited over foreplay.

Pumping my tongue into her, I played with her clit until she was screaming with the first orgasm I'd ever given her—the first of many. Only then did I leave that delectable mound to insert the part of me that had been wanting to be a part of her for so long.

I moved up her taut body, deliberately rubbing my skin against hers as she struggled to catch her breath. Cupping the back of her neck, I whispered in her ear, "Open your eyes, Julia. I want to see you when we connect for the first time."

She opened her eyes, which had gone dark with desire. She gripped my biceps then nodded. "Do it. I'm ready."

I kissed her once more then pulled back. "I will always love you."

"And I you." She let her lips part, her body looking totally relaxed and ready.

The head of my cock pulsed at the edge of her vagina. I could feel the heat coming from inside of her. The wetness of her juices would help me glide into her virgin tissue.

Our eyes locked, I could feel her body tighten as I slowly slid in the first inch before making one hard thrust, filling her with my rigid cock.

Her eyes went wide and one tear fell down her cheek. My heart ached to know that I had caused her any pain. I wiped it off her precious face, and then any glimpse of pain in her expression went away as we stared deeply into each other's eyes. I saw myself in her brown eyes. I was inside of her in more ways than one.

I was in her heart. I was in her brain. I was in her soul.

Moving slowly, I saw the pain had left her body completely, and all that remained was pleasure. She moved one hand up to place her palm against my cheek. "I had no idea, Artimus."

I couldn't take my eyes off her as I continued giving her long strokes that took me out of this world and into another one. She wrapped her legs around my waist; her nails clawed my back as she arched her body up, urging me to go faster.

Her innocence was no more, and she wanted more from me. So I gave it to her. The beast inside of me tore through, taking her with a savageness I didn't know I had.

She loved it, screaming wildly as I slammed into her. When her body went stiff, and her cunt clenched all around my cock, I burst inside of her as we reached our orgasms together. A bright light seemed to fill me as we came together that way.

I had never experienced the kind of heat that took over my body then. She held my shoulders, pulling her body up to mine, her breasts squishing against my chest as we both panted that same precious word to each other.

"Forever."

The End

Did you like this book? Then you'll LOVE Dirty Desires: A Bad Boy Billionaire Romance (Dirty Network Book 3)

Lost love can be hard to overcome, but maybe she can help me find my way back again ...

Her backside is what first caught my attention.

Round, firm, plump, juicy. Those are the words that ran through my mind when I first saw her bent over the table in front of me.

For a couple of years, she'd filled my fantasies, and now she was filling my dreams too.

But someone else had lived in my dreams for a long time. I didn't want her knocking that person out of my life forever.

Pushing her away seemed impossible. No matter how hard I tried, my arms kept pulling her back to me.

And just when I was able to let it all go, it all came crashing down on me again.

Had I been cursed? Doomed to live life without love? Or could she break that spell?

Start reading Dirty Desires NOW!

https://books2read.com/u/3ıxwp7

Lightning Source UK Ltd.
Milton Keynes UK
UKHW020247020121
376235UK00002B/86